To Sharon,
Enjoy!
Melody Gay

A SAFE HARBOR

by Melody Gay Berg

LAKE SUPERIOR PUBLISHING
Paradise, Michigan

LAKE SUPERIOR PUBLISHING
Paradise, Michigan 49768

In memory of Harvey Nason Berg Jr, whose love of Whitefish Point equaled mine, and Margaret Elizabeth Dantuma, whose love of writing inspired me.

ACKNOWLEDGEMENTS

To Luther, a captain in the truest sense of the word, who piloted me through many a storm.

To Wyatt and Shari, whose tireless efforts brought this project to its polished end.

Throughout the long process of bringing this book to fruition there have been several friends, old and new, who have contributed immeasurably. In addition to those already mentioned, I particularly wish to extend my gratitude to Anita Vollink for her advice and help with the early drafts, and to my son, Justin Berg, for encouraging me to write and revise. To the numerous others who encouraged me I also wish to offer my thanks. Please forgive me if I have neglected your names, and know that your support is appreciated!

A SAFE HARBOR

The night was still,
Ne'er a ripple and all was calm,
But alas, the sea awoke in an awful mood,
And woe to all within her reach.

What provoked this sleeping lady,
To cause the bravest to abandon arrogance,
And quote some forgotten psalm?

Truly the storm is against us,
And the waves are real,
But wiser are we from what they teach.

- Excerpt from "Storms of Life"
by Harvey N. Berg, Jr.

CHAPTER ONE

LAKE SUPERIOR lay sleeping in the warm July sun, not a ripple marring her vast body. Only when a freighter crossed her expanse did she toss and turn from the wake of the passing vessel, then once again settle down to her peaceful sleep.

A small sailboat lay nestled in her arms as seagulls glided overhead. The warmth of the afternoon sun beating upon her waters made the occupant of the tiny craft drowsy, and crawling into the cramped cabin, she lay down and fell into a deep sleep. The lone sailboat bobbed gently as it wandered farther and farther across the immense body of water.

Emily Kincaid had not slept for days. Her mind had been

too full of the events of the past few weeks, and of the incident that had changed her life and driven her out onto the lake today. Now she slept as one who had been drugged.

Slowly the sun set behind the horizon. Stealthily, as a thief in the night, indissoluble fog crept slowly over the lake, engulfing every vessel in its path with an impenetrable accumulation. Soon the tiny craft was also embraced by the misty thickness. Unknown to Emily, she was in grave danger.

The beacon from the Whitefish Point Lighthouse struggled to penetrate the fog while its high pitched foghorn sent forth its warning signal to all ships traveling around the point.

Several miles from the point the *Harrison P. Cambridge* made its way through the fog at a painful four knots. Captain Matthew Christian stood before the large windows of his ship, peering into the hypnotic denseness. The window wipers beat out a steady rhythm as they continually worked to keep the surface clean of moisture. First mate Henry Stone sat near the radar screen, watching the blips that appeared there. The thousand foot *M.C. Andrews* was ten miles behind, while the *C.W. Blackburn* traveled ahead. To first mate Stone's right was a map of the underwater

2

shoals hidden in Lake Superior. Occasionally Stone would study the map, giving directions and courses to follow to Wheelsman Thomas Smith. Smith glanced from the compass to the massive wall of fog surrounding the ship. All three men were seasoned sailors, putting in over eighty years amongst them sailing these great lakes. The radio crackled out messages from one ship to the other.

Captain Christian walked to the back of the bridge, and peering out the window couldn't see the aft part of the vessel. It was as if a giant knife had sliced off the back of the freighter, leaving only the pilot house. So thick was the fog, the lights on the aft were concealed. Captain Christian knew he was responsible for this seven hundred and fifty-foot freighter, and all twenty-eight men on board. Everything would be running as usual. The cook's helpers would be finishing the dinner dishes, while most of the crew that was off duty would be sitting around talking of adventures they had experienced on the lake. Others would be writing letters home or sleeping in their bunks. The engine room would be manned by the third engineer, an oiler, and one other engineer-type with perhaps less than an hour to go before the second officer would take over. Captain Christian himself would normally be off duty and in his cabin, but tonight, with the fog like pea soup, he was on the bridge.

The fog did not alarm him, for he had experienced this many times before. In fact, he welcomed it. It was like a security blanket wrapped around him, shutting him out from the world that lay out there. He felt he could hide from his past, and maybe even his future. Matthew Christian had just passed his fifty-ninth birthday. For thirty years he had sailed the Great Lakes. He knew nothing else. He was at home here. Lake Superior was more familiar to him than any other "lady" he had ever known. He knew her moods and tempers could change in an instant. She had always been the most remote and aloof of the upper Great Lakes. He had traveled a good share of her majestic three hundred and eighty-three miles. He loved her while others couldn't abide her. At this very moment he wouldn't trade places with anyone else. He was exactly where he wanted to be.

Moaning deeply, the freighter's horn bellowed out three short blasts. It was answered by three more from a passing vessel. This signal would continue until the fog lifted. It was an eerie sound that echoed across the water.

Emily Kincaid awoke with a start! Sitting up, she rubbed the sleep from her eyes. Rising, she left the cabin

4

and stepped out on deck. What greeted her stunned her! Nothing could be seen. Moist droplets clung to her hair and body. Panic swept over her, and she felt terror fill her soul. Her throat went dry, while sweat trickled down the middle of her back. Hurriedly, she switched on her vessel's running lights. Looking up into the blackness toward the *Lonely Lady's* mast, her eyes tried to focus on the light there, but the fog was too thick. She had to do something, but what? It was so easy to get turned around on the lake, and think you were heading one way, only to find you were going in the opposite direction. Emily froze as her ears picked up the sound of the wailing strain of a freighter's horn. Could she possibly be in the path of one of those giants? She turned the key on and pushed the button to start the *Lonely Lady's* small engine. The purr of the motor gave her confidence, but which way should she go? Slowly, she began to pilot the boat forward. She reached under the seat, produced a life jacket, and quickly put it on. She didn't even want to contemplate the possibility of going overboard. Lake Superior, she had read, had only two temperatures— solid ice and melting ice. She shuddered to even think about it.

"Calm yourself," she said out loud. She realized now how foolish she had been to venture out onto Lake Superior today with a broken compass. But in her despair she had felt the lake calling her and she had no power to resist it. She had longed for its comfort and solitude. When she had left the harbor it was such a lovely day, and she didn't think she would fall asleep, waking up to this. Her hands were shaking uncontrollably. Panic was creeping over her again and she wanted to scream, to run, but to where could she flee? She swallowed hard several times, trying to stay calm, but each blast of the freighter's horn caused her to jump! The sheer terror of her situation began to play on her mind and she became confused. Instead of sailing away from the sound of the horns, she was navigating closer and closer.

"Captain Christian, I'm picking up a blip to our port. It comes and it goes. It's the strangest thing. It's almost like a phantom ship."

Captain Christian stepped over to the radar screen and watched with Henry Stone.

"Radio the *Andrews* behind us and see if they pick anything up on their screen," Captain Christian spoke gravely. The answer came back negative. They saw nothing.

Then the blip just disappeared and was gone. When it reappeared on their screen several minutes later, the object was only one-half mile away and approaching.

"Captain, it's back!" Stone exclaimed.

"Blow the warning signal, Stone! Order all available hands on deck!" the captain commanded.

Silent feet ran up the stairs and over the deck to the enormous spotlights. Their beams shot forth only to bounce back, unable to penetrate the thickness.

"She is still approaching, Captain!" announced Stone. "We're on a collision course!"

"Notify the *Andrews* we're about to crash with heaven knows what! What idiot would be out there on a night like this, ignoring our signals? Is he drunk?" Captain Christian bellowed.

The ship came to life as every crew member scurried to their posts. Life jackets were donned and lifeboats were manned as they braced themselves for the inevitable.

When the seven hundred fifty-foot freighter *Harrison P. Cambridge* hit the *Lonely Lady,* it tossed her around like a tiny toy in a tub, smashing her into pieces. As the small craft deposited her solitary passenger into the waiting arms of Lake Superior, Emily's screams could be heard by the crew standing on deck.

CHAPTER TWO

LAKE SUPERIOR hugged Emily to her breast. Down she went, suffocating. If she didn't get some air her lungs would burst. Then, just as quickly as the lake had taken her, it released her. Bobbing to the surface like a cork, her eyes and nose full of water, Emily coughed, spewing liquid from her mouth.

One short, two long, one short blasted from the *Cambridge's* whistle, alerting ships in the area she was at a standstill. The deep wailing sound drove home to Emily's already over-wrought nerves. Screams escaped her lips, her arms and legs kicking and waving. Her continuous screams helped guide the rescue boat to her location. Crewmen Scotty King and Ernest Printing pulled her water-logged body into the small craft. Emily lay on the bottom, whimpering like a small child. A bright light shown onto her terror stricken face.

"Was there anyone else in the boat?" Crewman King asked. All she could do was shake her head "no" as she stared into the light, her eyes large and transfixed.

"Let's go, Ernie!" Scotty stated with a note of urgency.

Expertly, the craft was turned around by experienced hands toward the sound of the *Cambridge's* whistle. Three hundred yards from the ship Ernest Printing shouted out, "We have her, Captain!"

Cheers went up amongst the crew. The order was given to start the engines and prepare to get underway.

As they neared the *Cambridge* the grey fog glowed from its powerful spotlights. The lifeboat nudged the side of the huge vessel and took its position underneath the enormous chains that had lowered her into the water earlier.

The spooky sound of the cable lowering intermingled with the shouts of the crew. Hooks were fastened to the launch and the lifeboat was slowly moved up the black sides of the *Cambridge* to the top deck.

Captain Christian stood just outside the pilot house door. When he was certain all were safe on board, he gave the signal that slowly set the freighter in motion. Frothy white bubbles danced to the water's surface as the engines rumbled into action. All ships in the area were notified the vessel was back on course for Duluth.

Captain Christian paced the bridge, knowing the danger in which he had just put his ship and crew. He'd had no choice! Once he had hit the craft and heard the woman's screams, he had to stop. He could not leave her out there in that endless fog and water, doomed! Slowly, he began to calm down. He only hoped there were no more surprises awaiting him out there!

After turning the ship over to first mate Stone, Christian went below to check on his new passenger. He found her settled in the cabin next to his, sitting on the bunk, her hair tousled and wet. She had changed into a pair of oversized blue jeans and shirt that had been lent to her by Scotty. Scotty was cleaning a gash on her left cheek, and her left arm was visibly swollen. The scolding that had formed in the Captain's mind left him at first glance of her. She looked so helpless, afraid and alone. Green eyes, brimming with tears, looked into his. Her lips quivered.

Stepping to the side of Scotty, he quietly asked, "How bad is the cut?"

"Not enough for stitches, Captain, but it needs to be cleansed and bandaged."

Looking at Emily, he stated in a soft tone, "I am Captain Matthew Christian. You are one lucky lady!"

"I know," Emily said in a choked voice, lowering her head so the captain couldn't see her tears. "Thank you for saving my life."

"It was Scotty and Ernie who saved your life. Let me look at your arm."

"I don't think it's broken, Captain, just badly bruised." Scotty declared.

Captain Christian gently felt of her arm, his fingers searching for broken bones. Emily flinched, biting her lower lip to keep from crying out.

"Are you in a lot of pain, or only when I touch it?"

"A lot of pain!"

"Scotty, give her something for the pain and get an ice pack to put on her arm."

"Aye, aye, Captain."

Alone with her now in the cabin, the captain paused a moment before speaking to Emily again.

"I must notify the Coast Guard of tonight's happenings. Do you have a family member I can contact for you?"

Emily sobbed, "No... no one!"

Captain Christian's heart was touched by her words.

"Parents? A husband perhaps?"

She could only shake her head "no."

He ran his fingers through his short, wavy dark hair, turned from her and walked to a small table in the room. He had to get back to the bridge; he was tired, and irritable! At the same time, something was compelling him to stay with her.

Turning, he faced her once more. She sat slumped over, holding her arm. Tears cascaded down her cheeks and onto her lap. Sadness, mingled with pain, etched her face.

He reached into his trouser pocket, pulled out a white handkerchief, and handed it to her. She took it and wiped her tears and her nose.

Scotty arrived with the ice bag and some medication. Emily dutifully swallowed the medicine.

"Here, Miss, lie down. I'll put this ice on your arm and cover you with a blanket."

Scotty's voice was soothing, like a mother tucking her child into bed.

"The pain reliever will work soon and make you drowsy."

When Scotty had made her comfortable, he turned to the captain. "If you don't mind sir, I'll retire now?" Captain Christian nodded his head in approval.

Looking back at Emily, Scotty bid her goodnight and stepped from the room.

"I'll also leave you to rest," the captain said, "but before I return to the bridge, will you please inform me of the name of your boat, as well as your name?"

"The *Lonely Lady,*" she whispered. "My name is Emily Kincaid."

In the early hours of the morning the wind gently blew the fog away and revealed a black velvet sky studded with thousands of bright twinkling gems.

Fatigued, Matthew stumbled down the stairs to his cabin. As he neared Emily's room he paused and listened. Slowly, he opened the door and peered in. A lighted lamp hanging on the wall cast shadows across the room. He could make out Emily lying on the bunk, her breathing coming easily. Gently, he shut the door. He arrived at his quarters exhausted and flopped on the bed fully dressed.

Rising high in the sky, the sun shone brightly on Lake Superior the next morning. The wind had kicked up and the waves were dancing. The morning was well on its way to noon before Emily awoke. It took her several minutes to get her bearings as to where she was. Slowly the events of the previous night began to dawn on her. Her head throbbed and her arm pained her.

She sat up on the edge of the bunk and looked at her surroundings. The room was small, grey in color, and the lamp on the wall was still burning. A chair and table completed the furnishings. Hanging on the chair, dried and pressed, were her own clothes. She walked over to a door to her left and found a bathroom. It was small, but adequate. Gazing in the mirror on the wall, Emily was shocked by her appearance. Circles rimmed her green eyes. Swelling had puffed up her left cheek. Gently removing the dressings on her face, her fingers touched the tender spot. She flinched as she splashed warm water on her wound. She removed Scotty's oversized shirt and slipped into her own clothing. The red sweater and navy blue slacks felt warm on her shivering body.

A gentle tap sounded on the cabin door. Emily left the washroom, stood in the middle of the room, and bid them to enter.

Scotty peeked around the corner, his white teeth shining

in his ebony face. "Good morning, Miss. Did you sleep well?" he beamed.

"Yes, thank you, Scotty, I did. What time is it?"

"Almost noon."

From nowhere, the door of her cabin was full of crewmen trying to get a glimpse of the lady plucked from the lake. Scotty began to introduce them. "This is Pete, Henry, John, Floyd, Sam, Slim," and the names went on, until they became all blurred to Emily.

Laughing, she held her hand up in protest. "I will never be able to remember all of you."

They all seemed a good-natured bunch of men, laughing and trying to make her feel at ease. Sensing her discomfort, Scotty shooed them all away. They left with grumbles on their lips.

"How come you're privileged, Scotty? Give us a chance to talk to her too."

"Later, men, there'll be time," and Scotty pushed them out of the door, shutting it behind them. Smiling, he turned to her and asked, "Hungry?"

"Yes, but first, do you have a tooth brush? My teeth feel fuzzy this morning," she laughed.

"I figured you might need one," Scotty said, and

reaching into his shirt pocket he produced a brush, toothpaste, and a comb. "After you get cleaned up, take this hall to the first door, turn to the left, go down the long hall to the end. Go right, and that is the galley. I'll inform our cook, Frenchy, that you're coming. There will be a few of the crew there, as we're about to change shifts, so you'll not have to eat alone." Giving her a broad smile and wink of the eye, he closed the door and left her alone once more.

Her hair combed and her teeth brushed, she made her way to the dining hall. She had no trouble finding it, for the tantalizing aroma of roast beef filled her nostrils as she made her way through the passageways. Most of the men were already seated when she entered the room. All eyes looked toward her, bringing a blush to her cheeks. Talk stopped as she stood in the doorway.

Several of the crew jumped to their feet at the same time and came toward her. All talking at once, they asked her to sit with them. She was confused as to what to do, when Scotty entered and came to her rescue. Steering her to the table nearest the door, he seated her. He sat next to her like a protective mother. She didn't know that the captain had given Scotty orders to keep an eye on her. The captain knew his crew and knew them well. Most of them were married, but a few of them would take any woman to bed at the first chance they could get. The captain wasn't about to let that happen on his ship. He knew Scotty and trusted him. Scotty was a happily married man, with no thought of another woman. He would treat Miss Kincaid as he would a sister.

The table Scotty had chosen for them to sit at was, like all the other tables in the room, heaped high with mashed potatoes, gravy, roast beef, carrots and peas, salad and homemade breads. Coffee pots were stationed at several places on the table. She had read that the men on these freighters ate well. She could now attest to that. Heaping her plate full of good food, Scotty ordered her to eat. Conversation soon picked up between the men, leaving Emily to sort out her own thoughts.

One by one, the crew finished eating and left the galley, having lingered as long as they dared. Scotty called the cook, Frenchy, over to meet Emily. He was a warm and friendly man, short in stature and balding, with round glasses set precariously on his nose. As he spoke to Emily he beamed from ear to ear.

Emily praised him on his culinary abilities. He spoke in broken English, which delighted her. Scotty informed her that Frenchy was part French and part Canadian. He was a fixture on the *Cambridge*, for he had been with them for fifteen years.

"Would you like me to take you on a tour of the ship, Miss Kincaid?" Scotty asked.

"I can't think of anything I would like better, Scotty."

"Are you sure you're up to it? Do you need another pain pill?"

"No, for right now, I'm doing pretty well. My face is tender, but the air will do it good."

The two spent an hour touring the ship, traveling through halls, past bunks, cabins, heads, and down to the boiler room where the heart of the great vessel pumped life into its veins. The noise and heat of the confined area was suffocating to Emily, and she would be glad to go above and breathe in fresh air. But first they ventured deep into the belly of the Cambridge, walking along a tunnel that ran from stem to stern. Emily learned that this passageway was used during storms, allowing the crew to walk inside, safe from the elements.

Freighters are built to twist and turn with the forces of Lake Superior. As they walked down the eight by eight foot hall, Emily thought about the phenomenon called "hogging and sagging." She had read this was a common occurance in this part of a freighter. With so much movement in the hull, one second you could see all the way to the other end of the ship; the next second it looked like it was gone.

Lastly, Scotty took her to see the cargo hold where the taconite pellets were stored.

"Minnesota is the largest producer of iron ore in the United States," he explained. "Nearly all of the high-grade natural iron ore has already been mined there, but advances in technology have found a use for taconite, a lower grade iron ore. The taconite is crushed, processed into hard marble-sized pellets, and shipped to steel mills where the pellets are melted in blast furnaces and blown with oxygen to make steel. We'll be picking up a load in Duluth."

"Where will you take the pellets?" Emily asked.

"Detroit, Michigan," he replied.

Leaving the cargo hold, they entered a narrow doorway and ascended steep stairs to a recreation room where activities of various kinds were in progress. Some of the men were lifting weights, keeping their bodies firm and strong. Others were playing ping-pong, while the more studious men had a complete library at their disposal.

"The company that owns the *Cambridge* wants to keep

its men happy, so they furnish all these activities for us to make it feel like home," Scotty grinned. "I, myself, like to lift weights. Keeps me trim." He chuckled.

It was all very interesting but Emily was feeling a bit tired. Her arm was hurting, and she felt the need to sit down. As she made her way back past the galley she heard her named called. She turned to see who had spoken and looked into the open door. There she spotted the captain sitting at the table eating his lunch.

"Are you up to talking, Miss Kincaid?" he asked.

Emily paused for just a moment, then nodded her head "yes."

"Come sit down, and I'll have Frenchy bring you a cup of coffee."

She slipped into a chair opposite the captain, observing him as Frenchy set a cup of steaming coffee before her. Last night she had been in too much pain to remember what the captain even looked like. Today, in the light of day, she found him to be a very attractive man. Fifty was what she judged him to be. His height slightly taller than hers, she guessed he had a five-foot-seven frame. His complexion was smooth and tan from constant exposure of the sun. An old tune came to her mind as she gazed into his deep brown eyes. "Beautiful, beautiful brown eyes, I'll never love blue eyes again."

For a brief moment a sharp pain engulfed her heart as she thought of Paul, the man she had given her heart to only to have it broken. Paul's eyes were cold blue organs that held no feelings. But these brown pools she was looking into held many emotions; deep feelings flowed from them. The faint fragrance of his Old Spice lingered from his morning shave and filled Emily's nostrils with its pleasant aroma. Thick, dark, wavy hair, flecked with white, gave him a distinguished look. When he smiled she noticed a slight gap between his two front teeth. She found it a very charming feature that enhanced his entire appearance. As he raised his fork to his mouth, Emily observed his hands — strong, slender, tan hands with a youthful appearance. The pinky finger of his right hand was bent as if it had been broken and never set properly. She knew they were soft to the touch. The memory of them still lingered on her from last night.

So deep was she in observing him, Emily was unaware he was also regarding her. He deduced she was about ten years younger than himself. Chestnut hair framed her face and her green eyes held a note of sadness to them. The left side of her face was turning black and blue from her bruise, the cut open and raw. Her teeth were even and her lips nicely shaped. She was not what he would call beautiful, but somehow attractive. He was very much aware she was taking notice of him.

He had received information on her that morning from the Coast Guard. She lived at Whitefish Point, Michigan, and was under a government grant to study the changes in Lake Superior. She had no family, as she had stated the previous evening. But what puzzled Matthew was the sadness in her eyes. What was causing it? Something about her intrigued him!

Matthew pushed his empty plate away, took his coffee cup in his hands, and looked Emily full in the face. She began to blush. Captain Matthew found this unique. Most women today found nothing to blush about.

"Emily," he spoke in a soft tone, "do you mind if I call you Emily?"

She shook her head "no."

"Emily, what in the world were you doing on the lake last night in a fog like that?" His eyes held hers.

"It wasn't foggy when I set sail yesterday morning," she answered flatly. "I fell asleep, and when I awoke..." she paused, "well, you know the rest."

"Why didn't you use your compass to get you back to shore?"

She sat in silence a moment before she spoke. "It was broken."

"Broken!" he exclaimed in amazement. "You ended up in the shipping lanes! That's the most dangerous place you can be out there! You must know that." He almost shouted at her.

"Yes sir, I do."

"Then why didn't you have your compass fixed before you ventured out on the lake?"

Emily hesitated before answering. She couldn't allow herself to be vulnerable. How could she tell him of the hopelessness she had been feeling? Even she knew that it was out of character for her to be so careless. But how could she explain to him about the desperation that had driven her out onto the lake that day? The captain was waiting for an answer. What could she say?

"I just kept putting it off," she said.

He took a deep breath and then slowly expelled it as he rubbed his forehead. He was trying to compose himself before he spoke. "Emily, I've received news from the Coast

Guard that you're employed by the government to study the changes in Lake Superior. Surely, after studying this body of water, you are acquainted with her moods! You must know that it's vitally important to have a compass when you sail these waters—a working compass!"

A few moments passed and then he said in a softer tone, "Emily, what drove you out onto this lake yesterday?"

Slowly shaking her head from side to side, a tear fell from her cheek, onto the table. In a choked whisper she spoke. "I can't tell you right now. It is too painful. Please don't ask me! I can't bring myself to talk about it."

Too painful... oh, how he could understand those words. Didn't his own past keep coming before his face? It, too, was painful, gnawing at him and robbing him of the tranquility he so longed for. If she was experiencing even half the discomfort that he was, his heart went out to her. He wouldn't question her further. Did it matter why she had been out there? He would soon be at the Soo locks in Sault Ste. Marie. He would drop her off there, never to see her again. Let her keep her secret, as he had kept his locked in his heart. His "skeleton in the closet" had cost him the woman he loved. He lived in constant fear that someone would dig into his past and reopen old wounds.

"Go back to your cabin and rest, Emily," he said gently. "I won't be able to put you ashore until we're finished in Duluth and return to the Soo. Do you have someone who can pick you up there?"

She nodded "yes."

"Very good!"

Rising from the table, he left the room.

CHAPTER THREE

THE FAINT SOUND of a woman's scream piercing the evening air dragged Matthew Christian back from the depths of sleep. Again, a shrill cry reached his slumbering frame and this time he sat upright in bed. He grabbed his trousers, hastily put them on, and ran out of his cabin barefoot. As he reached Emily's quarters, three other crewmen were advancing down the hall. They burst into her room and found her sitting up, clutching the covers to her chest. Scotty's large shirt on Emily's small frame made her look like a fragile, frightened child. Large tears streamed down her face. She placed her hand over her mouth and tried to stifle the screams as she looked at the men standing in her doorway. Matthew made his way through the men and sat beside her. He placed his arm around her shoulder, drew her near, and spoke soothing words to her.

As they looked at their captain, all three men stood dumbfounded! Scotty was amongst the three and couldn't believe what he was seeing. In all the years he had sailed with Matthew Christian, he had never seen him with a woman. Each time their ship pulled into port or departed, their wives, sweethearts, mothers or sisters were there to kiss them good-bye and wave them off. No one was ever there for Captain Christian. Scotty knew that two years ago the Captain had lost his wife, but even when Mrs. Christian was living she never came near the docks. When all others were taking their monthly leaves, eager to be home with their families, Captain Christian stayed aboard. When Mrs. Christian had been ill and in the care of her sister, the captain would leave his ship and visit her, but never for more than a few hours. Two years had passed since his wife's death. Any other man would have found himself another woman by now, but not the captain. He was the best captain anyone could sail under. He never gambled, drank, or used colorful metaphors. Matthew was so different than most of the men he sailed with. Christian was special... unique, sailing one of the finest ships on the Great

Lakes.

Scotty wondered about the chain around Matthew's neck. He had never seen it before. The chain secured a gold ring dangling down his bare chest. Scotty contemplated the possibility it had once belonged to the Captain's wife and that he wore it now as a reminder of her. He couldn't remember the Captain ever talking about his family. He was a very private man, always willing to listen to the men about their home lives, eager to view the pictures of a newborn son or daughter, but never offering any information about his own personal life. He was indeed a loner. He treated the men with respect, courtesy, and was patient with all.

Scotty was brought back to the present by Matthew's words.

"Scotty, I think Miss Kincaid is all right now. You all may go back to your duties. Thanks for your concern."

They turned, one by one, and left the room. After the door was closed neither spoke for several minutes. Emily began to feel uncomfortable leaning against the captain's bare chest. She lifted her head and moved away from him as a blush colored her cheeks.

"I'm sorry, Captain. I was having a bad dream. I was on the *Lonely Lady* once again and your ship was coming upon me out of the fog. I woke up screaming."

"Are you alright now?" he questioned.

"Yes, thank you, I'm fine."

"Then I'll leave, but if you need me I'm right around the corner."

Back in his own cabin, he became restless. He put on his shirt, socks, and shoes, along with a light jacket, and went to the upper deck. The sky was covered with twinkling stars. A falling star shot out from the safety of its orbit and, streaking across the midnight canopy, fell toward earth. The celestial bodies were so much brighter out here on the open water, away from any street lights that would distract from their brilliance. A slight wind tugged at his hair. His ship was alight from stem to stern, penetrating the darkness.

Steadily, the *Cambridge* set a course through Lake Superior, leaving a wake to ripple and slowly find its way to shore. Bubbling white water was pushed away from her bow as she ploughed her path. Silently, another freighter slipped by, her hull ablaze with white lights like a string of diamonds floating on the water. It was always peaceful for Matthew to watch other freighters pass so quietly in the night. Under his feet the engines rumbled. The ship vibrated slightly.

Breathing deeply, he filled his lungs with good clean air. Matthew touched his shoulder. He could still feel where Emily's tears had fallen upon his skin. The warmth of her body next to his had given him a sensation he hadn't had for years. He leaned on the rail and looked out into the blackness of night. It had been so long since he had been that close to a woman. His mind couldn't comprehend the fact that, as close as he had been to her, she didn't find him repulsive as his late wife Millie had. He dared not think of a woman, let alone touch one. Yet she had lain in his arms, soft... tender. He had erased from his memory what it was to touch... to hold a woman. A shiver ran along his spine, for he knew he must not let these feelings enter his heart again. Millie had killed all those feelings in him. He must let them stay dead. If Emily had known about his past she wouldn't have allowed him to be so close to her.

No, his life was on this ship. This was his woman. He was married to her as surely as he was to any mortal. She was part of him. He knew her from stem to stern, loving her for her strengths and her weaknesses. He took care of her as he would any female he could love. He understood her every mood. He knew when to run her full speed ahead, or slow her to a crawl. He could bring life into her. He knew she would never turn from him and reject him as his wife had. His devotion and loyalty was so strongly bonded with this old girl that he knew, if the time came, he would go to the belly of Lake Superior with her.

CHAPTER FOUR

EMILY stood by the railing watching the morning sky sweep away the darkness of the night. A gentle breeze caressed the bruise on her cheek as the sun peeked over the horizon. With a tingle of excitement, she watched the Cambridge gracefully slicing through the water. Having picked up their load in Duluth, the feighter was now on its way back to Detroit. Soon they would be entering Sault Ste. Marie. Emily didn't want to waste a minute of her last day on the Cambridge.

Having spent every moment she could exploring the ship, talking to the men, and in quiet conversations with Matthew Christian when he was not piloting the ship, Emily had gleaned much information. The *Howard P. Cambridge* was well equipped, giving the men every comfort possible. Meals were almost gourmet, equal to many famous restaurants. The recreation room was always buzzing with activity, as was the rest of the ship, but yet it had a relaxing pace to its daily routine as well.

Emily wasn't sure which she liked the best — daytime, when she could stand by the rail with miles and miles of water surrounding her, the sun beating down, tanning her soft skin; or night, when the moon beckoned the stars out to shine like a thousand candles, the passing ships alight in their evening best, adorned with sparkling diamonds as they glided across silky waters.

When she shared her thoughts about the diamond lights with Matthew, he chuckled at her description. She was enthralled when he explained to her that at Christmas time each crew decked their vessels out in multi-colored lights, even producing a Christmas tree with all the trimmings. When Emily inquired if these ships sailed even on Christmas Day, she was informed that indeed they did. Christmas was spent with the ship's "family", for after traveling together for so many months they came to regard each other as such.

Gaily wrapped presents were placed under the tree for

each member of the crew to create more of a holiday atmosphere. Frenchy went all out to make them a traditional Christmas dinner of roast turkey with stuffing, sweet potatoes, several vegetables, various salads, home-baked breads and a large selection of desserts, such as pumpkin pie, Christmas pudding, cakes and decorated cookies.

* * * * * * * *

In her studies of Lake Superior, Emily had found that this lake was the queen of the five sisters. It was easy to remember the great lakes using the acronym H O M E S: Huron, Ontario, Michigan, Erie and Superior. None of the others had the disposition of Superior. When her temper was aroused her waves would pile up like mountains. She could strike with more deadly force than any storm on an ocean. Exploding, her anger racing across hundreds of miles of open water, she would lash out at any vessel in her path. If you were unfortunate enough to be found on Superior during one of her tantrums, you had no choice but to ride out her fury. Clamping her teeth into a vessel, shaking it like a dog would a limp rag, she could destroy it in a matter of minutes. Unlike her distant cousins, the oceans, whose waves roll and swell, the Grand Lady prefers to jump and tumble, twisting her body in grotesque contortions. Emily learned from one of the crew that it is a standard joke on the Great Lakes that salt-water sailors often become seasick on what they call our "inland ponds." For when they first sail on her grand body, they turn green in the face and position themselves by the railing.

The Lady's moods can change in an instant from a sleeping beauty queen to an evil, angry witch. Within the matter of an hour the temperature can dip to a winter chill or spring to a summer's warmth. Advance forecasts are not reliable because of her unpredictable nature.

Emily could tell by Captain Christian's talk of the *Cambridge* that he was truly in love with his ship. He was proud of her seven hundred fifty-foot length, which could carry a cargo capacity of thirty-one thousand gross tons of ore. The *Cambridge* was one of the older vessels still in operation. Christian was not ashamed of her age or the fact that her pilot house was positioned in the front of the freighter, while in the newer vessels the bridge is at the aft of the ship. Matthew had explained to Emily that when the *Cambridge* was empty her ballast tanks were flooded with water, thus lowering her to increase her maneuverability. The tanks would also be kept flooded during loading to keep the deck hatches level with dockside loading equipment. The freighter had a mark on its hull, indicating the level it should be for loading during the winter months and summer shipping season. He explained to her that the manner of loading and unloading them a century ago was now a thing of the past. Manpower was the main machinery then. The pellets were put in barrels and lowered into the cargo hold, or wheelbarrows full were pushed onto a plank, across to the freighter, and dumped into the hold. Needless to say, it took a lot of time and energy. To make the work quicker and more efficient, some vessels of the modern shipping industry were equipped with their own crane system for loading and unloading. For ships without cranes, Matthew had said, a man named George Hulett from Cleveland had invented an ingenious gadget called the "Hulett Unloader." It has a control cab with a man inside to operate the machinery. Attached to this control cab are two huge jaws like on a crane. These jaws are operated from inside the cab. The cab can go down into the hold of the ships and scoop up large amounts of taconite pellets, lift the closed jaws up and over the ship, and deposit them where they are needed. Needless to say, it takes only hours to unload, whereas before it could take days.

Emily inquired of Matthew as to why he and his crew dressed in street clothes instead of uniforms. She told him she had expected to see him in a navy blue suit, complete with brass buttons. Matthew threw his head back and Emily heard his laugh for the first time—a deep hearty laugh.

"That's a romantic notion, Emily. We're very informal on ship."

All these things Emily learned, but during her stay on the *Harrison P. Cambridge* she found out nothing about the captain. The only information Scotty could give her was that he was once married but now widowed, and nothing else. He was a very sequestered person.

When the *Harrison P. Cambridge* pulled into the Soo Locks, Matthew extended his strong hand toward Emily and waited. She slipped her smooth, feminine hand into his and looked deep into his fathomless eyes.

"Thank you for everything, Captain."

"You are welcome, Emily Kincaid."

He watched as she was lowered over the side of the freighter onto the sidewalk of the locks. Turning, she looked up at him and said, "I hope I haven't caused you too much trouble, running into your ship?"

"Not at all, it was..." and he paused, searching for the

right words. A mischievous twinkle lit his eyes. "It was adventurous!"

Pleased, she nodded and turned to leave.

"Emily," his voice stopped her. "On July twenty-third I'll be rounding Whitefish Point. I'll give you a salute: three long and two short on the ship's whistle. If you're there, you'll know it's me passing."

A smile crossed her lips. Turning, she walked away. He watched her until she was out of the gate and lost in the crowd... both still holding tight to their secrets.

CHAPTER FIVE

EMILY SAT DOWN on the green bench near the clump of birch trees outside her cabin door. She leaned back, soaking up the sun. This was her favorite spot. From here she could view all of Whitefish Point. To the right of her was the harbor and Brown's Fishery. Looking to the left, she took in the beach down to the point which jutted out into the water. Just behind her, the tip of the lighthouse could be seen over the tops of the trees.

A hint of smoke touched her nostrils. The sturdy brick kiln alongside the waterfront was processing the catch of the day, turning the delicate whitefish into a delectable mouthwatering treat. She had been in the fishery once, watching the men clean the morning's catch. The pungent odor of the entrails being cut from the fish caused her to gag, and she hadn't returned.

Emily chuckled to herself as she watched the seagulls greedily circling overhead, awaiting the remains of the fish to be tossed out to them. Hundreds of gulls would then dive into the fish entrails, fighting with each other for the biggest piece. Whenever the fishing skiffs entered the harbor, the screeching seagulls circled around the vessel, coveting the choice morsels. When there was no boat to hover around, these cocky birds would position themselves along the cement pier, just waiting for their next meal, only leaving if a human intruder would venture into their midst. Flapping their wings and screaming in protest, they would lift their bodies gracefully into the air and retreat to the other "break wall" where once more they would keep watch.

Emily recalled walking out on the pier early one spring to discover a large bird's nest built there on the flat hard surface. One lone large egg was nestled in the straw home. A young lad was kneeling by the habitation, examining it. Why would any bird build its nest there, when so much foot traffic came that way?

The egg remained cradled in the straw for several days, then it and the nest just disappeared. Not a strand of straw remained. "Isn't that just how life is?" Emily thought, "Especially here on the point." Each day she had observed the changes in Lake Superior. The color could change from a lighter gentle blue; the lake magnificient and calm, to a dark green — menacing, forceful and dangerous. For one brief moment a fleeting, fearful feeling walked across her heart.

Emily's eyes lifted to the harbor. Several boats were moored there. Boaters from other states often sailed their crafts through the Soo Locks and up to Whitefish Point as it was a favorite harbor for many sailors.

The beach was dotted with people, some lying close to each other on towels while their young children played in the sand. Others splashed in the bay. A golden retriever was jumping in the water, biting at the waves coming to shore. His tongue was hanging out of his wide open mouth, giving the impression he was laughing with sheer enjoyment.

A few people walked along the shore, stone scoops in hand, digging in the sand and rocks, looking for the coveted Lake Superior agate. Some wore hip boots, enabling them to walk out into the water and delve there for the precious stone. When polished, these minerals could be made into items of jewelry, such as cuff-links, bracelets, necklaces and earrings, in all different shapes, sizes and colors.

There was enough of a breeze coming off the lake to drive the dreaded black flies inland. Here it was bearable to sit, as long as there was a breath of wind. But go inland and the black flies would swarm the flesh of any living thing, biting into man and animal alike. Emily thought about how even this pesky insect couldn't drive the people away from this part of Upper Michigan. All who lived here would tell you that the beauty of Whitefish Point outweighed the troublesome pest.

Lake Superior was relatively calm today. Gentle waves lapped her shore, while the sun glistened off her body. As she looked out upon the bay, Emily's thoughts drifted to last night. Again she had been awakened by her dream. It was always the same. Down, down she drifted to the bottom of the lake, her lungs begging for air. She could see her body floating in the water, her hair flowing out around her face, her eyes bulging, as she tried to hold her breath. Paul's face would then appear to her, a cynical smile on his lips. It was always at this point she would awaken in a cold sweat, the bed covers soaked and rumpled. Slowly she would come to the realization it was only a dream. She could see his handsome face now; his blonde hair and blue eyes.

Two years ago she had met and fallen in love with Paul Spooner, a resident of Paradise, Michigan. Their friendship had started out simple, with each day bringing more meaning and feeling into their relationship. Each morning brought new significance to her life, and new things to discover with Paul. She'd had a purpose for living.

It had been a clear March day when he had driven to her cabin, and on the snow-swept beach, asked her to marry him. Her heart had burst with joy as she gladly accepted. She had kissed him good-bye with the promise they would be together that evening. She had watched him walk down the narrow path to his car, and waved to him until she could see him no more. There had been a spring in her step as she returned to her small abode. But soon the cold March winds would blow across her heart.

Evening came, with the shadows lengthening. The coming of this night was no different than all the thousands of nights before. But he didn't come. When Emily phoned his home there was no answer. She had driven to his residence only to find him gone. For days she tried to locate him, but her search was in vain.

Then one day she saw him in Paradise. She had run to

him, her heart racing with anticipation. When he turned to look at her, she knew he had changed. Gone was the love in his eyes, the soft tone in his voice. He looked at her, and with all the indifference of a stranger, said in a calm voice, "Hello, Emily." When she had questioned him as to why he had changed, what had happened and why he hadn't come to her home that night, he only looked at her with a blank expression and said, "It's over, Emily, I don't love you."

"How could a person change so quickly?" she had asked herself a dozen times. In the months that followed, her heart, body and soul had gone through a thousand changes. Shock took hold as she drove back home. Tears replaced the shock; buckets of tears. Numbness stole over her body and was gradually succeeded by a great empty void. Something had died in her heart that would never be reclaimed again. Death had crept in and settled over her like a heavy blanket. Feelings for everything and everyone had been snatched from her. She'd remembered reading about death. One no longer cries, hates, loves or laughs when death comes. It was as if she were deceased. Nothing and no one mattered to her. For her life had no future, just a deep darkness. It was as if she had fallen into a pit. She was sure she would never be able to crawl out.

The first day of her separation from Paul had left her by the phone, begging it to ring. She could not leave the cabin, even to walk along the beach where she could have found healing power, for fear he would call while she was out. It became an obsession with her to stay by the phone. Cold sweat would break out over her flesh as she would hurriedly take a shower, the entire time praying that he wouldn't call during this daily necessity. To sleep at night was impossible. Anxiety kept her awake, waiting for that all important call. She had become confined, a prisoner of her own making. She hoped he would be suffering as she was, enduring the same pain that was stabbing into her heart, spreading across her chest. One moment she hated him, the next she loved him.

It was only later she had found out he was already married, and had gone back to his wife. In broad daylight she could think about all these things with calmness, but at night he entered her troubled dreams.

Emily was brought back from her musing by the sound of a freighter's whistle. Turning toward the point, she saw a large black freighter just coming into view. It was hugging the shore, its mighty engines pounding. The ground underneath Emily's feet shook from this giant rounding the point. She always marveled at how these ships on water could cause the earth to tremble. Picking up her binoculars, she focused them on the vessel. She knew even before the name came into view what freighter it was. Again the whistle sounded... three long, two short! The people on the beach turned their attention to the point, shading their eyes against the bright afternoon sun.

Emily stood to her feet as the name *Harrison P. Cambridge* came into focus. A smile crossed her lips as she heard someone question, "I wonder what he's blowing his whistle for?"

Warmth crept over her as she reveled in the secret of the hidden message. She sat down on the bench again and watched the *Cambridge* until it became a wiggly line, a mirage in the hot sun.

CHAPTER SIX

EMILY'S RESEARCH took her to many parts of Upper Michigan. Traveling by car, she would venture to various locations to study the level of the water, how much the beach had eroded, and if the lake was going further out or coming in. It was exciting to her to study the charts and maps in her cabin, a task of which she never tired.

One of her favorite spots to visit was the Vermillion Station. It had received its name from the red ochre deposits near the shoreline. In the 1800's this stretch of coastline, located ten miles west of Whitefish Point, was home to a U.S. life-saving station. Emily found it an enjoyable spot to visit. She had read that many years ago the station had been washed out into Lake Superior during a storm. Then in 1938 and 1939 a new station was erected. In 1943 the station was abandoned. Later, it was sold to a party in Ohio who had plans to retain the building as a tourist attraction. But, as so often happens, the plans fell through. Vandals came and, along with the elements, almost destroyed the old landmark. The large framed station stood stark on the vast expanse of flat beach. On stormy nights the waves hungrily reached out for the staunch structure.

A caretaker, Clem Munson, had been hired to lovingly care for this watchdog of the lake. Clem felt akin to this decaying old building. For many years he had sailed these lakes while the Vermillion Station stood watch. Countless times the old sailor had passed these shores. When he had retired from sailing and learned that careless hands had been scarring the faithful landmark, he applied for the job of caretaker and received it.

Having married late in life, he moved with his wife and daughter, Jenny, to this desolate stretch of beach. Jenny was the apple of Clem's eye. He had purchased a horse for her, a white stallion she had named Lightning. Emily thought about Jenny now as she drove that narrow road through the woods to the station.

She came to a small bridge, crossed it, parked her car

alongside the building, and got out. Pausing a moment, she looked out across the beach. Many days Emily had found Jenny astride her horse, racing down this stretch of beach; Lightning's mane, tail and Jenny's hair all flowing out behind. When Jenny would ride over to greet Emily her cheeks would be red and her eyes alight with excitement.

Two years ago Jenny and her mother had died in a tragic fire. Clem was heartbroken but chose to stay on at the station. Shortly after Jenny's death, Emily had come to see Clem and found him watching Lightning racing down the lonely beach with no saddle or rider. Clem was bent over with his hands hanging by his side. Tears were streaming down his weather-beaten face and into his white beard. Emily had slipped her young hand into his gnarled weather-worn one and squeezed it.

"Do you want me to go after her, Clem?" she had asked.

"No Emily, let her be free. She's lonely for Jenny too. Let her get it out of her system. She'll be coming back."

But two days later Clem found her on the beach, tangled in some fishnet and lines that had washed up on shore. Lightning's leg was broken. Later, with tears in his eyes, Clem had shared with Emily how difficult it had been for him to make the decision to put the horse down. All this went through Emily's mind as she stood gazing down the beach.

"Morning, Clem." She surprised him as she walked up behind him.

"Well, Emily, good day to ye, Girlie! Ye be in time for a cup of coffee."

Emily smiled to herself as she listened to Clem's soft New England accent mingling with his quaint, old-time "salty sailor" dialect. She had questioned him about it once. He chuckled as he explained, "It be with me all my life, Girlie. Guess I picked 'er up while sailing!"

After Clem had lost his family, Emily made it a point to visit him often just to check up on him to make sure he was doing okay. Nothing could persuade him to leave this part of the country. He had sailed on many ships, on all of the Great Lakes. Emily loved to sit and listen to him tell his tall tales. What fascinated her the most were the scrapbooks he had kept. His grandfather, who had started the collection when he was a captain, had handed them down to Clem. Clem had added his own clippings to the books. Every shipwreck on the Great Lakes that had been published in the paper was in these albums. Little notations, made in the margins with Clem's own scribbly handwriting, added a special flair to the contents. These were his prized possessions. He loved to sit over a cup of coffee and share them with anyone who was interested.

Emily and the old captain had spent many enjoyable afternoons together, talking and pouring over his treasures. He had helped her many times with her research and in turn Emily had helped him through a most difficult time. Once a month Clem would ask Emily if she would drive him to the cemetery located along the shores of the lake. There he would stand by the grave of his loved ones and talk to them. Emily would leave him to his private talks, wander around the burial ground, and read the tombstones. It was a quaint graveyard with trees growing over the tops of many of the graves. It was not on flat ground, but lay in the humps and hollows of a hill. Some of the graves that extended up the hill had low white fences surrounding them, while others were graced with low, black, ironwork barriers. Artificial flowers poked into the rough hard ground added splashes of color to the otherwise rustic landscape. Gently, the sound of waves coming onto shore drifted up over the hill to the tiny mounds while the wind rustled the leaves on the trees. This resting place for many loved ones was so different from the manicured lawns of the city plots. Emily found it the loveliest cemetery she had ever seen.

Clem would spend half an hour with his wife and child and then return to Emily with the words, "I feel better now, Girlie... thanks."

As Clem and Emily entered his house she could smell the aroma of fresh brewed coffee.

"I stopped by, Clem, to invite you to go to the Soo with me in a couple of days. Care to go?"

"By gum, Emily, I think I'd like that!" he said with a twinkle in his eyes.

"Good, I'll pick you up on Thursday at eight o'clock. Too early, Clem?" she teased.

A toothless grin spread across his face.

"Now Emily, you know I'm up before the birds. I'll be ready and waiting!"

After spending an hour with Clem, she left. Driving back to her cabin, her mind was on Clem and the loneliness he must endure. She could sympathize with him. She was feeling lonely herself.

CHAPTER SEVEN

EMILY had to stifle a giggle when she picked Clem up on the following Thursday morning. His slight frame was clad with an antique navy blue captain's uniform. The brass buttons had a dull green finish to them. The pants were shiny from many ironings. As he eased himself into her car the musty smell of the old trunk where the suit had been stored still clung to his garment. The scent of mothballs struggled with the cherry blend tobacco descending from the pipe clenched between Clem's teeth. The mothballs were winning!

"Good morning, Clem, beautiful morning!" She spoke cheerfully.

"Morning, Girlie! It is a lovely day!" He spoke with a

merry gleam in his eyes. "Did you see the sunset last night? 'Red sky at night, sailor's delight,'" Clem mused with a chuckle.

Laughing softly, Emily finished the proverb for him, "Red sky in the morning, sailors take warning!"

They continued to chat as they drove down the tree-lined pavement that followed the shore of Lake Superior. Soon the beauty of the day cast a spell and their thoughts drifted, each on their own charted course.

Emily's mind was on the task that was taking her to Sault Ste. Marie. It was there she turned in her monthly reports of the lake changes. She was confident in her job but always a little uneasy when turning in a report. She worried that maybe she would leave out something important. As she drove along in silence her mind went over every detail in her account.

Clem sucked on his pipe while his mind wandered to the past when he was a captain sailing the Great Lakes. How he missed those days—the feel of the wind in his hair with his feet planted firmly on the deck, and the mist on his face on a foggy night. How he'd love to feel those things again.

He had envied Emily's jaunt aboard the *Harrison P. Cambridge.* When she had told him about it he had hung on every word. His old mind couldn't comprehend all the newfangled equipment they had on board a ship now. Why, they were almost like a luxury liner compared to what he sailed on in his younger days. By gum, what he wouldn't give to go aboard one of those vessels.

He glanced at Emily and, sighing inwardly, felt concern over her heartache. He was glad Paul was out of her life but he didn't like what his leaving had done to her. He knew from the moment he had laid eyes on Paul Spooner he wasn't the one for Emily. He knew Emily was not a young lass anymore, by some standards. The years were clicking away for her as they were for him, only in a different way. Women and men married young in life, yet he himself had married late. Tears came to his eyes as he thought of his Bessie, and Jenny. Black-eyed, black-haired Bessie — how happy they had been. And when she had presented him with Jenny he'd thought his heart would burst. Now they were both gone. But he had found happiness for a little while and he hoped this woman next to him would find happiness again.

Sunlight drifted through the dense trees along the road. Birds sang in the pines, while squirrels scurried from tree to tree playing peek-a-boo. Lake Superior would make her appearance from behind the trees, her waves rolling in great swells onto the flat stones lining the beaches. Then it would disappear from view as the trees once more concealed her.

Emily and Clem passed Iroquois Point Lighthouse. It was standing white in the afternoon sun, its doors open to passersby, inviting them to climb the steep stairs to the beacon's tower and gaze upon the breathtaking view of Lake Superior. It sat in all its glory on the Chippewa County bluff, its light marking the division line between Whitefish Bay and the western end of the St. Mary's River, which connects Lake Superior and other Great Lakes.

Emily remembered reading that by 1620 Iroquois Point had become a familiar landmark for French explorers such as Étienne Brûlé and Grenoble. They were the first recorded white men to come to this area. Fur traders and missionaries followed, making Sault Ste. Marie the first white settlement in what later became known as Michigan.

The Point Iroquois Light was built on the point's highest ground in 1856 and included a dwelling for a full-time light keeper. Only eleven years later a government inspector questioned the construction quality and laid the ground work to replace it. Following the American Civil War, a decision was made by the United States Lighthouse Board to create a lighthouse lifesaving station building on the Great Lakes.

In 1870 the light was torn down and replaced with the current Point Iroquois Light. This new light and keepers' quarters became a focal point of the shoreline lumber community of Brimley, Michigan. In 1885 the bell tower was erected, which used a Stevens automatic bell-striking machine. Emily often wondered how that might have sounded. She envisioned it sounding similar to a church bell. She wondered if that sound had become inadequate and may have led to the decision to tear the bell tower down in 1890 and replace it with a fog signal building with steam whistles.

In 1905 a two-floor extension was added, providing living space for three lighthouse keepers. During its peak operation the keeper's children and local fishermen were enough to populate a local school on the grounds for a period of time. There was also an assistant keeper's quarters, a fog signal building, three barns, a chicken house, boat house, oil house, outhouse and well-house. It wasn't hard for Emily to let her imagination run wild and to step back in time, imagining in her romantic mind what it was like to live as a lighthouse keeper.

It wasn't until 1962 that the station was deactivated and

replaced by the Canadian operated Gross Cap Reefs Light, an unmanned buoy-type beacon in the St. Mary's River channel.

Emily never tired of seeing the faithful structure, with its white exterior and red roof. Basking in sun, the beacon stood strong along the shore, overlooking the sparkling waters that lead to the Soo Locks. She had climbed its tower on more than one occasion, breathing in the fresh air. Every time she walked through the lighthouse museum she learned something new of the history that lay on the shores of Lake Superior.

After arriving at Sault Ste. Marie, Emily left Clem at the Soo Locks while she conducted her business in town. After finishing her task she returned to the locks and parked her car in front of the souvenir shops. She stepped out of the car, then paused to look at the row of stores huddled shoulder to shoulder and inviting everyone to enter their doors. She could never resist doing so, and entered the nearest establishment.

The shop was true to its name. Everything on display was embossed with "Sault Ste. Marie, Michigan." Dishes, placemats, tee-shirts, billfolds and wall hangings all carried the name. Many displayed pictures of the giant freighters that entered the locks, while others just showed the locks themselves. Emily smiled to herself as she witnessed many little hands clinging to precious finds that would likely be broken before they ever reached home. Indian moccasins, tomahawks and headbands with colorful feathers occupied one corner of the shop. Banks in the shape of freighters were stacked in neat rows, awaiting the hands of a souvenir seeker. The smell of cedar drew Emily to the cedar boxes, cedar chips in bags and cedar blocks to tuck in dresser drawers. This exhibit interested her most. The smell was so crisp and clean.

As she left the shop she looked down the long sidewalk at all the postcard stands in front of the stores, each of them displaying colorful cards of freighters, the Soo Locks, and various other points of interest in the town. She knew from past experience it was hard to pick from all these attractive cards.

The sidewalk was crowded with tourists, some sitting on the benches provided for those who needed to rest their weary feet. One man caught her eye. His wavy dark hair caused her heart to flutter. At first glance he reminded her of Captain Christian, and at that moment something stole over her—a premonition that the captain was near. Looking up and down the street she only saw unfamiliar faces. How could he be here when he was sailing the Great Lakes somewhere? She shook her head slightly and walked across the street where she encountered one of the ladies standing outside the information center. The woman was handing out leaflets about various restaurants on the strip. Politely, Emily took the coupons given her and entered the information building. She found it crowded with people looking at the brochures in the racks lining the walls. Others studied the scale model of the Soo Locks in action.

Emily strode to the racks and scanned the pamphlets on various topics of the Soo. She selected one on the history of the locks and then directed her steps to the blackboard on the back wall. She scanned the board for news of the freighters coming up-bound and down-bound, and for what time they would arrive. Her eyes froze on the second name on the board: up-bound, the *Harrison P. Cambridge,* at one-fifteen today. She checked her watch and realized it would be an hour before the vessel came through the locks. Emily left the building and walked down the flower-strewn sidewalk to the locks themselves. The observation deck, high above the locks, was filled with people viewing a ship that had just entered the gates. A large chain-link fence kept all from the edge of the locks but was still open enough to give everyone a good view. She found a bench along the fence a little ways from the observation deck and sat down. Clem was nowhere in sight so she opened the pamphlet she had picked up at the center and began to read the history of this fascinating invention of man.

It was hard for Emily to imagine back to the 1800's when Lake Superior was connected to the St. Mary's River by rapids only. Then, the only way for boats to enter from the river to the lake was by land around the rapids. She wondered how teams of mules and oxen could pull a large vessel, empty or full, on greased poles around the rapids by land. She felt sorry for the animals who had worked so hard doing all that heavy pulling. If the ship was too heavy with cargo it had to be unloaded and dragged across land, taking from six weeks to three months to complete, before it was reloaded and allowed to enter the water again to journey on. Today, with the locks in operation, this same procedure takes about an hour. All that hard labor came to an end in 1855 when a man named C.T. Harvey built the first lock. It was such a success that more locks followed, creating a boom in the shipping industry. Four locks were now in operation. The first American lock was named after General

Douglas McArthur. It is the smallest—only eight hundred feet long. The second was named *Poe*, after General Orlando Poe of the United States Army Corps of Engineers. This lock opened in 1969, being twelve hundred feet long and requiring twenty two million gallons of water to rise to the upper level of Lake Superior. The third lock, the *Davis*, and fourth, the *Sabin*, are also American locks. A fifth lock is owned by Canada and is also in operation. Across from the locks a building similar to a control tower at an airport directs all ships into each appointed lock. It was amazing to Emily that these locks all worked by gravity. No pumps are required to fill and drain the chamber for the ships to enter. Tunnels running under the locks either open or close to fill and empty, raising or lowering the water 21 feet to the level of either Lake Superior or the St. Mary's River. Only then would the giant steel gates open wide to release the ship. Shipping season only lasts from March through December, closing earlier only if the locks become too encrusted with ice. Reading further, Emily discovered that the locks are drained in the winter. During this time the locks are checked for damage and repaired.

Emily was so deep in thought she didn't notice another freighter approaching the locks until its whistle unexpectedly announced its arrival. All standing near jumped with the sound, followed by a ripple of laughter, each individual chuckling at themselves with a nervous titter. Emily was startled as well and joined the crowd in laughter.

As it eased its large hulk into the narrow enclosure, Emily could see the pilot house and the American flag flying proudly. The name of the ship was not visible to her, but only to those standing high on the observation tower. Silently, the freighter glided into position before the iron doors closed behind her. Slowly, like a sea serpent rising from the depths, the vessel emerged from its confinement. Standing by the chain-link fence, Emily watched as the name *Harrison P. Cambridge* came into view. At the wheel stood Thomas Smith, and peering down from his high perch was Matthew Christian. Stretching taut, the massive ropes creaked under the strain of the ship as they clung to the moorings on the dock. Walking toward the wheelhouse, his black complexion glistening in the sun, was Scotty. Leaning against the rail, he looked out over the crowd.

"Scotty... Scotty!" she yelled as she waved.

His eyes caught her figure behind the fence and his face broke into a broad grin.

"Emily! Emily Kincaid! How are you?" he shouted back.

She raised her arm and moved it up and down to indicate she was doing fine.

"Hey guys, look who's here!" Scotty motioned to the crew walking on board. One by one they came to the port side of the boat to greet her. They were all talking and laughing at once. The crowd turned to watch the scenario taking place. They seemed curious as to who this woman was and how she knew the crew of this freighter.

Turning to the bridge, Scotty cupped his hands around his mouth and shouted, "Captain... Captain! Look what I found!"

The door of the pilot house opened and the captain stepped out. His dark hair sparkled like the sun dancing on the water. A crisp, white shirt and dark slacks accented his trim masculine figure. Hands on the rail, he leaned slightly forward, peering down upon the crowd. When he spotted her a smile crossed his face. At that moment something tugged at her heart. What was so charming about him, she wondered? Her thoughts went back to something she had once read about a famous Russian actor whose gleaming white teeth were accentuated by a slight gap between his two front teeth. When asked why he didn't replace that tooth, he replied, "The women find it charming." Emily found Captain Christian's smile very enchanting. This went through her mind as their eyes held each other's.

"Hello, Emily, how are you doing? Is your arm better?"

"Yes, thank you, Captain. It's much better."

"And your face?"

Touching her face with her fingers, she smiled, "Healing nicely."

"Been sailing lately?" he asked with a smile.

A delightful laugh escaped her lips. "No, not lately, Captain. I received your salute on the twenty-sixth as you rounded the point," she called to him.

Throwing his head back, he laughed a hearty deep-throated laugh. "I wondered if you were there."

Emily had been on his mind a great deal since he had put her ashore. Without thinking, he inquired, "Emily, I have a few days' shore leave coming. Could I come to Whitefish Point and visit you?" The minute he asked the question he was uncertain whether he should have or not. Had he overstepped his bounds? Would the rejection now come? Emily stood still behind the fence, her face a blank.

"Aye, Captain, she be glad to have ye visit her," Clem answered for her.

Swinging around, Emily faced Clem and he gave her a

wink.

"Clem, when did you get here?" she demanded.

Turning toward Matthew, he stated, "My name is Clem Munson. Sailed these parts twenty years ago. Ye be Captain Matthew Christian, I presume?"

"That's right, Captain Munson." Clem beamed visibly as Matthew addressed him by his title.

"Perhaps I've put Miss Kincaid at a disadvantage, inviting myself to her home." Captain Christian said. Turning toward Emily, he spoke, "I ask for your forgiveness, Miss Kincaid."

Emily could read the hurt in his eyes and the fear of rejection in his voice. But she didn't want to become involved with another man — not for a long time, if ever! Life was just beginning to flow through her body again. She didn't want another disappointment. Something told her to say "no" to the captain, that he couldn't come, but her heart was telling her differently. What would it hurt if she said yes? They could be friends, couldn't they?

The ship had been rising slowly and now towered over her so that she had to look up to the bridge. "I would like that, Captain. When will you be coming?"

Relief erased the furrows in his brow. "I'll send you a

note announcing my arrival. I must go now." With a wave of his hand he entered the pilot house.

Scotty and the rest of the crew had become busy retrieving the ropes, and as the *Cambridge's* horns gave one short blast the massive doors of the lock opened and Lake Superior welcomed the iron ore carrier.

CHAPTER EIGHT

A HEAVY DRIZZLE descended upon the Upper Peninsula of Michigan. Clouds laden with moisture hung low, their billowy bags straining under the weight of their load. Matthew's car wove its way down Sandy Lane toward Emily's home. Splashes of purple, white, and yellow wildflowers were nestled in the thick forest floor, adding a dash of color along her driveway.

He pulled up to the back of her cabin, turned the key off and sat for a moment, drinking in the landscape. Everything was covered with mist. The trees dripped with dampness and the rain had turned the sand a dark caramel color. As Matthew opened the car door to step out he could hear the waves of Lake Superior thundering onto shore.

Emily was inside inspecting the neatness of her cottage for the last time. Since receiving Matthew's note telling her of his coming she had been busy cleaning and baking, awaiting his arrival. The interior of her home sparkled and smelled fresh. She had put clean linens on the spare room bed, laundered and ironed the curtains, and washed the windows. She was sorry the room he was to occupy was small, housing only a bed and dresser, but she felt the views made up for it. The back window looked out onto the woods, the wildflowers growing in profusion, and the blueberries, which were abundant this time of the year. Another large window looked out to the north, and she knew he would enjoy this view the most, for here he could watch the ships pass silently around the point.

Emily's bedroom in the loft had beautiful views as well. When lying in bed she could see all the ships traveling by day, and at night she could view their lights strung out upon the water. It was here the early morning sunlight greeted her, streaming across her bed and onto her face.

A slight knock on the door brought her out of her mental checklist. Crossing the wooden floor of her kitchen, Emily passed the large oak table and chairs and took a deep breath before opening the door.

They both said, "Hello," at the same time, followed by a laugh from each.

"Come in please, Captain." She spoke with a lilt to her voice. Stepping back, she allowed him to enter. Having closed the door behind him, she spoke again. "Let me take your coat, it's rather damp out there." She hung his coat on a peg beside the back door. "Did you have a hard time finding my place?"

"Not at all. As a matter of fact, with your directions it was very easy. The flowers along the drive are beautiful. I'm fond of flowers, but don't get to see them often, as I'm always on the ship."

"Are you tired or hungry from your long drive? Would you like something to eat, or perhaps a cup of coffee?"

Hesitating for a moment, he spoke. "A cup of coffee would be fine. I may have something to eat later."

"Make yourself at home while I fix it. The bathroom is down the hall and to your left. Your room is just across from that, if you care to freshen up."

The captain picked up his bag and disappeared down the hall. A few moments later he returned and stepped to the large double glass sliding doors leading out onto the front porch. He stood with his feet apart and his hands behind his back, looking out onto Lake Superior.

"It seems so strange to be on land, and not on a rolling ship. I guess I have to get my land legs back again." He chuckled. Emily brought him a cup of coffee, handed it to him, and retreated to the couch.

"It has been so long since I have taken a leave from my ship," he continued, "I had almost forgotten what it was like. It seemed strange to be driving a car instead of piloting a freighter, yet it felt good."

"How long has it been since you took a leave?" Emily asked.

"Two years, when my wife died. Not since." His voice was flat.

"Was your wife ill long?" It came out in a whisper.

He turned and then sat in the chair next to the window. In a very quiet voice he answered her. "Yes, Emily, she was sick a long time."

Silence filled the room, and Emily was almost sorry she had asked. She didn't know what to say next, for she could sense he didn't want to talk about his wife. It was as if he had gone back into the past, so deep in thought was he. Changing the subject, she inquired about his ship.

"Who is sailing the *Cambridge* while you're gone?"

He looked up at Emily as if he had just seen her for the first time. "I am sorry, I didn't hear your question."

"Who is taking care of the *Cambridge* while you're gone?" she repeated.

"An officer named Charles Post. He's an ageless old coot with experience. I trust the old girl with her. He's a relief captain, and works for my company. If the need arises he is there to fill in. I'll miss the old girl this week. Almost feel lost without her. But I'm glad for this leave."

"I hope you don't mind," Emily said, "but I have a full calendar for us while you are here. The blueberry festival is being held tomorrow in Paradise, and Clem Munson made me promise him I would bring you over to his place so he could chew the fat with you," she said with a smile.

"I don't mind in the least. Clem seems to be quite a character, just from what I saw of him at the Soo. Where did you meet him?"

Emily explained her friendship with Clem, how they met, and the bond that was between them now.

"Emily, I hope I have not inconvenienced you by coming here. I forgot my manners when I invited myself to come for a visit."

"Put your mind at ease Captain, I have been looking

forward to having some company. That day at the Soo, I wasn't sure of what I wanted. But I think a little company will brighten up this cabin."

The evening shadows soon began to creep in. The time flew as they talked of many things, but the subject of Matthew's wife did not come up again.

Emily had prepared a light supper of tossed salad, fresh whitefish, and baked potatoes for the two of them. After their meal, Matthew helped her with the dinner dishes. The evening was spent in leisure as they talked of hobbies and of their work.

Later that night, with the moon shining through her bedroom window, Emily had been sleeping soundly when the troubling dream came creeping into her slumber. Once again she awoke with sweat trickling down her back, the bed clothes rumpled and damp. She sat up in bed and waited until her eyes could focus on objects in her room. Slipping out of bed, she eased her arms into her terry robe and softly descended the stairs to the kitchen.

Matthew found her sitting there at the table, head in hands, elbows resting on the table top, her hair a disheveled mass of curls. He stood in the hallway, unsure if he should speak or remain silent. He had slipped into his trousers and padded out to the kitchen in bare feet. The gold chain with a ring hung around his neck and fell on his bare chest.

"Are you okay, Emily?" He spoke in a voice thick with sleep. He had heard the muffled cry that had come from her room upstairs, and then her soft tread on the wooden stairs.

Shaking her head without lifting it, she moaned, "Oh Matthew." He caught her use of his Christian name, but she didn't realize she had used it. He pulled out one of the chairs and placed it next to hers.

"Were you dreaming about the night you hit the *Cambridge?*"

"Yes... yes, I was. But there is always more to the dream than just when I collided with you."

"Do you care to tell me about it? Sometimes it helps to tell someone." He urged gently.

Emily wasn't sure if she should relate the rest of her dream to him. But then something inside told her that if she could tell anyone, it would be Matthew Christian. She felt he, too, had a deep burden he was carrying, and if he could release it he would be the better for it. So, slowly, she began to share with Matthew about her relationship with Paul, their breakup, her imprisonment in this cabin and finally her escape to the *Lonely Lady*. By the time she had finished she felt spent.

Matthew reached for her hand in the moonlit quarters, placed his strong, slender hand upon hers, and squeezed it.

"I am glad you told me, Emily," he said gently.

"Oh, Matthew," she sobbed. Laying her head on the table, she let loose the tears that had been locked up in her heart. Slowly, with hesitation, his hand rested upon her hair and gently stroked it.

* * * * * * * *

Morning dawned and sunlight filtered into her room. Birds sang from the treetops and she could hear voices from outside. Last night's conversation with Matthew came plainly to her now as she lay awake. She remembered his tenderness, his comfort during the raw moments when she had poured out her heart to him. There was lightness in her spirit today, and she felt like singing. A great burden had been removed from her shoulders. Last night was the first time she had spoken of it to anyone, except Clem. Today was the beginning of a new life for her—she could just feel it. She longed to be up and about.

After a refreshing shower, she clad herself in a pair of yellow summer slacks and a cotton knit top of many pastel colors. Her hair shone from the fresh shampoo and hung in waves around her face. Matthew's door was closed when she entered the washroom, and as she left the room she found it was still closed. Emily wondered if maybe she had kept him up too late last night.

Emily retrieved her white sandals from the closet and slipped them on her feet. She walked to the back door and flung it open to reveal the smell of a new day. The sun shone, filtering through the trees, as people combed the woods around her property, hunting for the luscious blueberries that grew wild in abundance there. She had posted signs to discourage these pesky pickers, but to no avail. It seemed as if they couldn't read! Today was the blueberry festival, and these folks were hunting the wild fruit to turn into pies and muffins to be sold there. Emily didn't relish the thought of purchasing her own berries later in the day.

The berries grew on low plants nestled on the floor of the woods. They were small in size compared to the cultured berries in the city, but their taste surpassed any grown on a farm. Emily grabbed a small bucket from a hook just outside the door and marched into the woods to gather her own crop, and to shoo away the intruders in her back yard. Just at the edge of her driveway stooped a man. He was gathering Emily's berries. She was about to speak with a sharpness on her tongue, when the man turned and looked at her. It was Matthew! She threw her head back and peals of laughter escaped her mouth.

"Matthew, I thought you were a stranger out gathering my harvest!"

"I couldn't resist! I haven't picked blueberries since I was a kid." He grinned.

Emily laughed so hard tears ran down her cheeks. With a surprised look on his face, he asked, "What are you laughing about?"

"Oh ... Matthew ... if you could see yourself." She chuckled. "Your lips are purple!"

A sheepish grin crossed his face and he broke into a bellowing laugh. "Emily, you have caught me. I'm afraid I'm eating more than I'm putting in my container."

They took a vote and decided to eat breakfast in Paradise at the Wild Blueberry Festival. The town hall of the small village was packed with local folks and tourists alike, all partaking of the scrumptious fare before them. Blueberry pancakes, blueberry syrup, breads, cakes, muffins and blueberry pies, along with sausage, eggs and toast were on the menu. An elderly gentleman walked among the throngs of people playing tunes from the 1940's and 50's on his well-worn violin.

At ten o'clock the Great Alfredo and his wife performed a magic show. Chairs had been positioned in front of the stage for the children to sit and watch his amazing tricks of illusion. Emily and Matthew found a seat near the back and enjoyed an hour of hilarious fun! The Great Alfredo called Matthew up to help him perform one of his many tricks. Emily couldn't help but think how handsome Matthew was standing there on stage, his curly hair, black as coal, with just a touch of gray at his temples. His smile, so genuine, showed the small opening in his front teeth. He carried himself well, his body firm and trim from constant workouts in the ship's recreation room. His dark complexion was complimented by the white turtleneck shirt and dark brown slacks he wore. His shoes were polished to a high degree, probably spit shined. He certainly could have any woman he wanted just by his looks, Emily mused.

She watched as Matthew took a pair of scissors and cut the red tie the Great Alfredo was wearing. She held her breath and hoped the trick would be a success. Each piece he cut was placed in a bag. When he had finished he handed the scissors to Mrs. Alfredo while the Great Alfredo said some magic words over the bag, then instructed Matthew to reach in and pull out the tie. The audience gasped and clapped, as Matthew pulled out a whole red tie and handed it to the magician.

Outside, many booths had been set up, displaying the handmade crafts of local artists. Pictures, painted rocks, painted sweatshirts, copper pots, Indian beads, wind chimes, polished agates and driftwood arrangements were all on sale. One picture had caught Emily's eye. The artist had captured a clipper ship in full sail being tossed at sea. In the center of the picture was a phantom head of an old sea captain, cap on head, pipe in his mouth, staring out to sea. She stood for a long time admiring that picture, and she and Matthew discussed it at length before they passed on to another table.

They left the town hall and drove the short distance into Paradise. The village was as busy as a bee hive. They spent the rest of the day browsing in Ruth's Gift Shop, Paradise Bakery, and lastly, the Cozy Corners, which was Emily's favorite. She always looked forward to entering this store and spending a few moments conversing with the owner.

Their day now at an end, they slowly walked back to the car. Both were so filled with thoughts of their day together, and the pleasure of each other's company, that neither felt the need to speak.

Leisurely, they made their way down the Tom Brown Memorial Highway to home.

CHAPTER NINE

WILD ANIMALS roamed the vast territory of the Upper Peninsula, and Whitefish Point was no exception. Graceful deer nuzzled their soft lips into the cooling water of the lake, drinking their fill. Clumsy bears waddled down to the water's edge to refresh themselves. Bobcats slinked through the thick foliage of the forest, and moose plowed their way through the woods and out onto the beach, their gangly babies following along behind. Snakes slithered along the woodland seeking a place to warm themselves in the late afternoon sun. Canadian geese strutted along the beach, regarding the point as their new-found home.

Emily and Matthew strolled along the beach, stones crunching underfoot. Large flocks of geese leisurely walked ahead of them, pecking at the sand, sauntering over to the water's edge, and then gracefully gliding in, their silent feet paddling them into motion across the water. Their brown bodies bobbed along effortlessly as they rounded the point.

An old abandoned house stood watch over the lake, its sturdy structure defying any storm to destroy its frame. The roof was naked of shingles. Gaping holes told of shiny window panes once housed there. Rotting fish net cluttered the degenerated floor, and mingled with it were beer cans thrown upon the heaps of netting by careless human beings. Standing tall, but shaky, an old look-out tower remained upright, keeping its vigil over the surrounding area.

Emily and Matthew found a driftwood log resting in the sand and sat down to watch as night slowly nudged day over the horizon. Both were content with each other's company; they spoke not a word. Only the waves breaking upon the shore could be heard. The lights from the harbor shone through the darkness as the beacon from the lighthouse slipped across the water.

Thousands of stars were scattered across the black velvet sky, as if God had taken a hand full and sprinkled them there. Blinking red and green lights flashed from a plane flying high above the couple. A gentle breeze ruffled

Emily's hair.

The silence was broken by the sound of a freighter's engines — a beating heart, pounding out a steady rhythm. Off in the distance, lights were visible from the Canadian shore.

"It's so peaceful here," Matthew breathed. "I could sit here all night and take in the beauty surrounding me."

"I'm so glad you came, Matthew."

"So am I, Emily... so am I."

His hand rested on the log and slightly brushed hers, but she didn't move. He dared not venture to pick her hand up in his and hold it. He was content for the moment that it was resting against hers. Emily had not withdrawn her hand, but had chosen to leave it there, slightly touching his.

Time passed quickly, each day full of new discoveries. Emily took Matthew to the Tower of Paradise. While drinking in the beauty of the landscape below and the sparkling body of Lake Superior off in the distance, she felt a pang pierce her heart, knowing their time together was coming to an end.

They thrilled to the beauty of the Tahquamenon Falls, as the water cascaded to the river below. Walking the well-marked path through the woods to the lower falls, they stood on the very edge of the mighty force as it threw thousands of gallons of root beer colored water over its brink each minute. They rented a canoe and paddled the waters surrounding the falls, getting wet from the spray thrown from the gushing torrent.

Matthew's last day with Emily was spent at Clem's. For the old captain, it was the highlight of his week. Emily had baked Clem's favorite cake — chocolate, with chocolate frosting. He grinned from ear to ear when she presented it to him. Coffee was brewed, and Clem's kitchen became a quiet harbor for two captains, each telling of their own experiences on the Great Lakes.

Emily sat in a corner watching the two men; Matthew sitting straight and tall, while Clem's well-aged body bent over the table, his pipe clenched between his teeth. She listened to them talk of storms they had battled and of ships they had sailed. Names rolled off Clem's tongue, as he lovingly showed Matthew his treasured books of ships wrecked on the Great Lakes. The *James C. Carruthers, Wexford, Argus, John A. McGean, The Bradley,* to name only a few. As Emily listened to their voices mingling, she couldn't help but notice that each wreck was during the months of October and November. Clem mentioned the big blows of Lake Huron, November 1913, the Lake Superior storms of November 1913, Lake Erie's Black Friday of October 1916, Lake Michigan's Armistice Day storm of November 1940, and November 1958 when the *Carl D. Bradley* went down. Each lake held its own disaster. Emily wondered why the owners of these large vessels, knowing these lakes were so unpredictable during these months, would risk the lives of the crew and take the chance of losing their freighters, along with all the cargo they were carrying. Was it greed that drove these ships out onto the lake, or the necessity to supply people with the cargo they carried? Probably Emily would never know. Yet she knew as sure as she was sitting there, that the captains and crews of these giants would take the risk during the coming winter months. It was in their blood and would remain there until the day they died. She also knew that most of them would be willing to go to the bottom of any of these waters before they would abandon their first love. Hadn't Captain Matthew Christian himself stated that he would go down with his ship, for she had served him well? "Why," Emily pondered, "Why would anyone be so loyal to an object that couldn't return any sentiments?" She guessed she would never understand this breed of men.

Emily and Matthew's last evening together was spent sitting on the green bench in front of her cabin overlooking Lake Superior. The stars were shining and the moon cast bright lace patterns on the dark water. The waves gently washed to shore, sweeping over the stones and bathing each one to a glossy shine.

Matthew spoke first, his voice deep, but soft. "I can't remember when I've had such a relaxing time."

"I was afraid I had dragged you to too many places," Emily replied. "We were busy every minute."

"I didn't mind," he said. "This shore leave has done a world of good for me. I've enjoyed being with you. This time with you has put life back into me." He breathed deeply of the fresh air.

"It... it's been good for me too, Matthew." Emily stammered, afraid of the feelings rising in her breast. Something was pulling her toward this man, feelings she had never felt for Paul or anyone else before. She couldn't put her finger on it, but they were there. She wondered if Matthew was feeling something of the same.

He stood and walked a few steps from the bench.

Thrusting his hands into his pockets, he watched a freighter silently slip past the point, its lights laying smooth upon the water.

"Emily," he said with hesitation in his voice. "Emily, would you mind if I wrote to you ... kept in touch?"

He didn't turn to look at her. His heart was beating rapidly in his chest. If she said no, he didn't want her to read the disappointment on his face.

Emily left the bench and went to stand beside him. She placed her hand on his arm. "I would like that very much, Matthew. Tomorrow will be a very empty day with you gone."

He turned slightly and looked into her face, moonbeams showing him her every feature. Since the night he took her aboard his ship, she had invaded his thoughts. He knew her face like he knew the back of his hand. He enjoyed looking at her, taking in every detail of her face, because he didn't know when he would see her again. He longed to press his lips to hers, take her in his arms and hold her, but was afraid to do so. He didn't want this enchantment that was weaving around them to be destroyed. It had been so long since he had kissed a woman. Those longings to hold a female had come so often at first, as he lay in his cabin at night, the emptiness creeping in. But he had learned to push them to the back of his heart until they came less frequently and then stopped altogether. But since Emily had crashed into his life, those feelings were surfacing again. He had thought that Millie, his wife, had crushed all these emotions, but he was wrong. This woman beside him was arousing these sensations, these longings that had lain dormant for so long.

"It's late," he said, "I have a long drive ahead of me tomorrow. I'd better retire for the evening."

Reluctantly, they walked back to the cabin.

CHAPTER TEN

WHEN PAUL left her, Emily had felt desolate, for she knew he wouldn't be coming back. Life had ended for her several months ago when he walked out, but now Matthew Christian had brought life back to her.

Matthew's departure had left the cabin feeling very empty and Emily's days long, but she knew she would hear from him again. The anticipation of hearing his voice over the phone, or perhaps reading his handwriting on the ship's letterhead, filled her days with a warm glow.

When she finally did hear from him it was in a much different form. A knock sounded on her door two days after his exit. Upon answering it, she found a UPS man standing outside with a large, square, flat package in his hands.

"Emily Kincaid?" he asked.

"Yes."

"This is for you, then," and he handed her the box and left.

As she took the parcel into her living room, Emily wondered who had sent it. The address on the outside was one she didn't recognize. Upon opening the flat box she discovered the picture she had admired at the blueberry festival—large waves tossing a clipper ship, while the ghost captain looked on, his pipe in his mouth. A note was attached that simply said: *"Thanks for the lovely week together. – Matthew C."*

She picked up the picture and danced around the room, hugging it to her heart. "Oh, Matthew," she breathed. Emily found a hammer and nail and hung the picture in the living room where she could gaze upon it and think of him.

Between visiting Clem, and her work, Emily kept busy. In the days that followed, Matthew called each time he anchored in port and the two wrote letters to each other. Emily was always at the Soo, with Clem by her side, whenever the *Cambridge* entered the locks. The mail bag would be extended on a long stick from the freighter and deposited on shore. Another bag would be exchanged with the mail that was to be carried by the freighter. Every bag interchanged contained a letter for both Matthew and Emily. Emily would stay by the locks and watch until she couldn't see Matthew's ship anymore, then turn and slowly make her way back home. Safe in her own cabin, she would read and re-read his letter, and the very same day begin a new one to him. When he received her envelopes they would be bulging with pages of news.

Emily had received a phone call from him when he had pulled into Wisconsin. Matthew informed her that on his return trip he had to make a short stop at a plant in the Soo to unload some steel. It was a favor to the company and not something he would ordinarily do, but in doing so he could spend a few hours with her. She was to meet him at the park along the St. Mary's River. He would have Frenchy pack a picnic basket and they could spend time there together.

The late September day was perfect for a picnic beside the river. Clem was invited to join them and gladly accepted. It was the middle of the week so the park wasn't crowded. Tables were scattered throughout the small picnic grounds and Emily chose one near the water, where she could watch for Matthew's coming. Sugar Island lay just across from the park where a ferry transported cars and occupants from one side to the other. It was here that the large freighters had to pass to reach the Soo Locks. So close were they in this narrow passage of water that Emily felt she could reach out and touch them. Their monstrous forms loomed way above the spectators on shore. The passage was so narrow Emily wondered how they could possibly sail through without scraping the bottom or the shoreline. Each passing vessel would blast a signal from its whistle, the deep resounding boom shattering the peacefulness of the people lingering there.

A small speed boat approached the shore. Matthew and Scotty were on board. Emily waved them over to her corner of the park. After stepping from the small craft, Matthew collected the wicker basket resting in the bottom of the boat before he shoved Scotty off. He flashed a smile as he walked toward Emily and Clem. Extending his hand to Clem, he spoke to him first. "How you been, old timer?"

"Just fine, Matthew! By gum, it's good to see you again!"

"You also, Clem!"

Then, turning to Emily, he stated, "I've only a couple of hours before I have to be back."

Emily could detect something was on Matthew's mind—something he wanted to say to her. She wondered if she had made a mistake bringing Clem along, for she was sure Matthew wouldn't talk in front of him.

Frenchy hadn't left anything out of their picnic. There was fried chicken, potato salad, pickles, olives, lemonade, and a cake for Clem. Clem's eyes lit up when he beheld the chocolate creation. "By gum, Matthew, did you have this specially made for me?"

"Sure did, Clem!" Matthew chuckled.

Frenchy had even found a checkered red and white tablecloth for them to put down on the table. Paper plates and cups, along with napkins and utensils, were tucked in the bottom of the basket. Matthew and Emily talked of incidentals while eating their fill. Emily could detect Matthew was a little nervous about something. Clem must have sensed it also, for when he had finished eating, he stated he was going to walk around the grounds. After Clem had left, Matthew stood up and began to clear the table.

"Matthew, is something bothering you?" Emily asked.

He stopped collecting the dirty plates and stood with one foot on the bench of the table, his arms crossed and resting on his knees. He hung his head before he spoke.

"Emily, there is something I must tell you about myself. Something you must know. Something I haven't told another soul about since it happened. To be truthful with you, I am scared to tell you for fear of what your reaction will be."

"Tell me Matthew... please," she pleaded softly. She could see he was struggling with how to start.

"It happened a long time ago. At the age of eighteen I was a deckhand aboard an ocean-going freighter. I then transferred to a Great Lakes shipping line. I skipped my way up the chain of command from wheelsman to third mate, then second mate to captain. I was twenty-seven at the time. I was young for a captain but I had learned a lot about ships from my grandfather. While taking my training to become a captain I met my wife, Milicent Strong, whose father was Bartholomew Augustus Strong II, owner of a large shipping firm on the Great Lakes. Millie's father gave me command of one of his freighters. I was on top of the world with a good woman to come home to when shore leave rolled around, and a magnificent ship to sail. I had been in command of Strong's vessel for six months when a tragedy befell me. It was a night enshrouded in fog, much like the night we collided. I was near the Straits of

Mackinaw, piloting the *M.C. Strong*, which was named after Millie. I was downbound and the Norwegian freighter *H. B. Bergstrom* upbound. We couldn't see each other except by radar. I was sounding my signal: three short blasts for ships traveling in the fog. The foreign vessel was sounding its horn, but not as often as required.

Old Bartholomew Strong was a rich man, but he had obtained his wealth by his penny-pinching ways. The radar hadn't been working properly on my ship and he had skimped, as usual, and neglected getting it fixed. The night I was sailing it wasn't working as it should. The *Bergstrom* would appear on my screen, then the radar would quit working and go completely dead. We had to navigate by compass and hope the captain of the other ship would hear our signal and return with his. As you well know, it can become confusing during the fog. You think you're going one way, and in actuality you are going in the opposite direction.

The fog broke just enough for us to see the Norwegian vessel cutting across our bow right before we hit it broadside. I received a blow to the head and was knocked unconscious for a few moments. When I came around, men were running everywhere. Lifeboats were being put over the side and lowered. I was dizzy and trying to clear my head. The *"Mayday"* distress signal was sent forth and help was on the scene in a short time." Here Matthew paused and swallowed hard. He walked away from the table and collected his composure. Returning, he continued his story.

"Several of my men died that night. I was taken to court for neglect. In fact, it was the radar that was at fault, but old Bartholomew wouldn't admit to anything. The case dragged on for two years before it was decided. I was to have my license taken away for one year. Strong had to pay millions of dollars in settlement to the families of the deceased. I was Bartholomew's scape-goat. The entire blame was put upon me, and not the fact that his stinginess had caused the accident.

It was a blow to Millie, and from that day forward she hated me... despised me! In her eyes I had brought disgrace to her family and destroyed the ship that bore her name. All I heard was what an incompetent captain I was, and what an unfit husband I had become. Her words held only bitterness and hatred. She was out to ruin me... to make sure no other woman would ever want me, even though she didn't want me herself. After hearing her words repeated over and over to me, I soon began to believe what she said. My self respect hit an all-time low.

I finally moved out and stayed with my grandfather. He was the only one who believed in me. When my right to pilot a ship was taken from me, he sent me away to Germany. He had a friend there who owned a shipping business and I took command of a ship there. I changed my name from Marcus Crippton to Matthew Christian.

I had received two visible marks the night the *Strong* foundered. The first, a scar along my left cheek. While in Germany I had some surgery done on it. The other was this finger." Matthew lifted his right hand and Emily beheld the bent pinkie finger. "This never healed properly and has remained crooked ever since."

Silently, an upbound freighter squeezed itself through the St. Mary's River, its black smoke rising to the bright blue sky. Absorbed in his thoughts, Matthew wasn't aware of its passing.

"Before I left to go to Germany my grandfather gave me a gift."

He pulled the chain with the ring from the inside of his shirt, slipped it from his neck and handed it to Emily. It was a gold ring with an engraving of a wrecked ship on its face. The bright sun bounced off its shiny surface as Emily moved it between her fingers. In small letters underneath the sinking ship was the word *Mataafa*.

"*Mataafa*... what does that mean, Matthew?" she questioned, as her face lifted to his.

"It's the name of a freighter that was wrecked on November 27, 1905."

There it was again... Emily thought, *another storm in November*.

"On the twenty-seventh of November, in 1905, the *Mataafa* left Duluth Harbor towing the 366 foot barge, *Nasmyth*. After traveling for several hours the captain had to make the decision whether to go forward or turn back. The seas were raging that night. Temperatures were dropping, snow was falling, and ice was forming on his vessel. He knew he couldn't battle it much longer; the two ships wouldn't make it. Towering waves washed over the ships, encasing them both in a deadly casket of ice. The captain gave the order to turn around and head back for harbor. Two other ships were ahead of him and one was smashed onto the pier during the violent storm."

Matthew continued on, telling Emily how the townsfolk came down to the pier to watch in the freezing temperatures, building bonfires to help guide the mariners to safe harbor.

The captain of the *Mataafa* realized he wasn't going to be able to tow the *Nasmyth* with him, so he gave the life-threatening order to cut her loose. She and her crew would have to find their own destiny in eighty-mile-an-hour winds.

The *Nasmyth* rode out the storm safely. With seas crashing over her, her anchors had held fast. Black smoke billowed from the *Mataafa's* stack as she re-entered the harbor at Duluth. While thousands watched on shore, their faces reflecting horror in the light of the bonfires burning brightly, Lake Superior picked up the frail craft and held her motionless before tossing her onto the side of the north pier. Screaming in anguish, the *Mataafa* was plucked out of the raging water, hung motionless for another split second, then smashed onto the opposite pier. In a matter of seconds she was broken in two as she rose high once more and was brought down with the final death blow onto the rocks. Lake Superior's icy fingers continued to reach out to the ship, as her bitter-cold tongue coated it with freezing rain and snow.

With faces etched with disbelief and shock, the residents of Duluth stood watch through the night, helpless to give assistance to the crew on board. The fires burning brightly on shore gave no warmth to their hearts as they prayed for loved ones onboard. Not until morning was a rescue crew able to reach the wreck, where they found the captain and a few survivors huddled together in the pilot house. For many years after this tragedy, *Mataafa* cigars were made bearing a picture of the doomed vessel. Sailors traveled the Great Lakes with stogies in their mouths that had cigar bands on them depicting the drama of that night.

"My grandfather was among those who witnessed that catastrophe, helpless to do anything," Matthew said. "Being a sailor himself, he respected the power of the Great Lakes. He had this ring made to commemorate the event. After that he never sailed again without it. When my ship, the *M. C. Strong*, sank he gave it to me and told me to wear it as a reminder that accidents can happen to any good captain. I've worn this ring ever since." He slumped onto the bench, spent.

The sun shone full on Matthew's exhausted figure. Neither he nor Emily spoke for several minutes. A few seagulls screamed overhead, looking for any morsel of food left behind. Emily could see Clem, his bent form standing farther down by the edge of the river, feeding the seagulls. As usual, the seagulls were fighting over who was going to get the biggest piece. Turning to Matthew, she saw the agony in his face. He was drained from the telling.

"Matthew," she asked, "what happened to your wife? Did she ever forgive you?"

He snorted out a choked laugh. "I tried to keep in touch with her but she wouldn't have anything to do with me. As far as she was concerned I was dead. When I heard she had been put into the care of her sister, I went to see her. I wanted to make things right with her, to seek her forgiveness. For some reason that was important to me. It had been so long since we had seen each other that she didn't recognize me. When it came to her who I was, her mouth brought forth curses and disparaging words. They rained upon me like a violent storm. In her sight I was still no good and never would be. She had destroyed all my confidence in myself and made me see myself as an undesirable. I went to see her several times before she died but she continued to curse me until the day of her passing."

Emily remembered Matthew telling her his wife had been sick a long time. She now knew what he had meant. It wasn't just physical illness, but sickness of the mind. She had let bitterness and hatred destroy her.

"Matthew, why did you feel you had to tell me this story?"

He reached for her hand across the table and looked deep into her emerald eyes.

"Don't you see, Emily? I wanted to know if, after hearing my story, you would turn away from me as Millie had. If you find being friends with a murderer unbearable, I want to know now, before I get back onboard ship."

Gently placing her hand over his, she looked at him with tears in her eyes.

"Matthew, you are not a murderer. What happened was an accident. It makes no difference to me what's in your past. What only matters is the future.

"Emily, no one knows this story but you. When I came back, as I said, I changed my name and appearance. I received a job with this shipping firm when I was thirty-five. The company in Germany gave me a good recommendation and my present company was glad to get a captain with such a good record. If only they knew! I've worried every day of my life that someone will find out. That's why I've chosen to stay onboard, never taking leave, until I met you. When we were at Clem's looking at all his scrapbooks, I knew it would only be a matter of time before he put two and two together. And what then?"

"Matthew, does it matter anymore?"

"Captain! Captain!" Scotty called from the small craft hugging shore. "Departure time!"

Matthew waved his hand in acknowledgment to Scotty. Turning back to Emily, he looked deep into her eyes before he spoke.

"Emily, there is so much I want to say to you, but I don't have the time. I must go!"

Emily handed his ring back to him. He pressed it back into her hand. "Wear it, Emily, for me."

"No, Matthew, you must keep it as long as you sail these waters. It's your good luck charm from your grandfather."

Nodding his head, he slipped the chain around his neck and let it drop underneath his shirt. He turned abruptly, and with long strides walked to the waiting craft. They waved to each other until the boat became a speck.

Emily went in search of Clem. After finding him, they sat on the grassy shore and waited for the *Harrison P. Cambridge* to slip its huge hulk through the St. Mary's River. Towering above her, its black stack belched out stygian smoke. Matthew appeared for one brief moment to wave to her in passing.

It was merciful that Emily couldn't see into the future. For if she had, she would have seen the "gales of

November" beating relentlessly against a black vessel, a ship fighting desperately to remain afloat, struggling to reach a safe harbor. But Lake Superior, queen of the lakes, wouldn't be satisfied until its captain and crew appeased her anger. They would succumb to her power and slip to the depths of her soul.

CHAPTER ELEVEN

"EMILY! Emily, Girlie! Be ye not listenin' to a word I say?"

She jerked her head around to face the old sea captain and looked surprised. "What, Clem? What did you say?"

"I say, ye be not listenin' to a word I say!"

"Oh... I'm sorry, Clem. My mind is elsewhere."

"Be it on Matthew?" he spoke softly.

They were seated in Clem's cozy kitchen, drinking black coffee.

"Yes, Clem," she smiled. "It be on Matthew."

"Does his past bother you, Girlie?"

Emily blushed. "His past, Clem? Do you know about his past?"

"Aye, I do, and if it be what you are thinking, don't hold it against the man."

"What do you know about his past?" She inquired.

He arose slowly from the table and walked to the bookshelf where he kept his scrapbooks. Taking one that had a well-worn cover, he returned to the table and placed it before her. He flipped through the pages, now yellow with age, stopped at one, and pointed to an article. The headline jumped out at Emily.

CAPTAIN OF ILL-FATED
STRONG FOUND NEGLIGENT

"Oh, Matthew," she whispered. "Oh, Matthew!" She didn't want to read it, but the page was beckoning her to do so.

"Clem, how long have you known about Matthew?"

"Ever since the day you brought him here, when we sat right at this table and talked of our ships and our travels on these waters. It be when I turned to this page that I saw a look in Matthew's eyes. It be the look of a haunted man. When ye left, I read this article and began to put the pieces together. I be sure the day we spent in the park, and I saw that look again in his eyes. I knew he had to tell you. That be why I took a walk that day... so ye could be alone with him.

"You've known all this time, but never said a word?"

"That be right," answered Clem.

"Matthew was afraid you'd find out and wondered what would happen." Emily spoke, her voice full of emotion. "He likes you, Clem. He really does."

"Aye, Girlie, and I like him. I can remember the sinking of the *Strong* as if it happened yesterday."

"Oh, Clem, tell me about it, please." She begged.

"I always felt the boy was done in. Lots of folks be thinkin' the same as I did. Bartholomew Augustus Strong was a very rich man, very shrewd. He got his riches by stepping on anyone that got in his way. He be as stingy as the day is long. He would scrimp on anything just to save a buck, even if it meant cutting short on safety for his ship and crew. When she hit the foreign vessel that night, the *Strong's* radar was not working. I believe that with my whole heart. The young lad spoke the truth when he testified of that in court. But old man Strong wasn't about to take the blame for the loss of lives or the wreckage of his ship. No sir! There was only one man he could put the blame on ... his son-in-law. The captain is the first to be questioned. And Strong had enough money he could buy anyone off, even the judge. Bartholomew bribed the judge to give Matthew a light sentence. Even though Bartholomew had to pay a large settlement to each family of the deceased, the actual blame was placed on Matthew's young shoulders."

Emily sat enthralled by Clem's story. Tears pooled in her big green eyes for the young captain who had to face charges of guilt when he knew he was innocent.

"There was one thing Old Bartholomew didn't count on. He figured it would all blow over in a few years, and the name of his son-in-law would fade from the lips of the talebearers. Millie, his only child, having just enough of her father's disposition, entwined with being spoiled, turned her back on her young husband. To her, Matthew was a failure, and she wasn't about to let him forget it. She felt, as sure as she was born, that Matthew had put a scar on the family name."

Emily began to form an image of Millie in her mind, and what she conjured up was not a pleasant picture.

Clem continued. "Bartholomew wanted a grandson desperately, and Millie, being his only child, would have to be the one to present him with an heir to the Strong fortune.

He didn't count on Millie turning against Matthew from the day the *Strong* sank. She never let Matthew visit her bed again. As the old proverb says, 'What goes around comes around.' Bartholomew could have told his daughter that he was actually to blame. But after seeing how she treated her husband, he was afraid she would turn against him if the truth came out. In the end, he paid dearly for his dishonesty. He had no heir. Clem paused and then said, "I always believed the young Captain Matthew had been set to drift with no place to anchor."

"Don't you think, Clem, that most people have forgotten what happened all those years ago? Is Matthew's concern for the past still valid?"

"Well, Girlie, it be like this. When the court made its decision, Matthew went to each family of his crew and begged for their forgiveness. The death of his men weighed heavily on his heart. It would have been better for Matthew to have gone down with his ship than to have lived."

"Clem, how can you say that?" She demanded.

"Because, Girlie, it be like this. When there has been a shipwreck and there are survivors, they always question the Almighty as to why their lives had been spared when the lives of their friends were snuffed out. There is guilt taken on by them, an unjustifiable guilt. With the help of friends and family, this can be overcome. But ye must remember, Matthew didn't get that support... only from his grandfather. Millie never let him forget it as long as she lived."

"I see," Emily breathed with a heavy heart.

* * * * * * * * *

September gave way to October as the stately green garments of the trees were exchanged for royal robes of flaming reds, blazing oranges, and dazzling yellows. Across the bay autumn colors set the Canadian shoreline on fire.

Gardens were harvested, leaving the soil dull and bare. Cans and freezers were filled with the bountiful crops. Burning leaves scented the crisp air. Sharp axes cut into piles of wood, splitting them into smaller chunks for the coming winter months. Snow shovels were brought forth and snow blowers oiled and repaired, in anticipation of the large amounts of snow soon to arrive. As November tucked October into her winter bed, a cold damp rain began to fall, subtly changing to snow.

It was a late November day when Emily awoke with the wind howling around her cabin. Unmercifully, it shook the trees like rag dolls and rattled the windows and doors. As she watched from her window, a large tree by her driveway snapped and she heard the crack and thud as it hit the ground. Waves lashed at the pier, driving high into the air like giant geysers. The entire shoreline was covered with rolling waves. Cold hard rain pelted against the window pane. Emily looked out the window and gasped. Never had she seen Lake Superior so angry.

Matthew had called her a couple of days earlier from Minnesota, informing her he would be sailing around the point today, and then on to the Soo Locks. Emily peered out into the storm, scanning the horizon for waves resembling "Christmas trees", the jagged outlines of swells, but found none. Instead, gale-force winds were blowing the tops off the waves. She had studied Lake Superior enough to know that when the "Christmas tree" waves were missing and the lake was taking on the form it had today, it was the sign of a full force storm. It was a body of water in mass confusion — "the gales of November."

After pulling on her blue jeans and heavy blue sweater, Emily flipped on the radio and listened as an announcement was made that winds of seventy-miles-per-hour were gusting and schools and businesses were being closed. All were advised to board up their homes to prevent shattering glass.

The wind and sand bit into her flesh as Emily struggled to the shed to retrieve the wood to board up the windows. Cold rain drove its way to her bones as her numb fingers fumbled with the nails.

The *Harrison P. Cambridge* was only miles from Whitefish Point, battling the heavy seas, trying to reach a safe harbor. If they could just make it to the point they could find security there. The *Cambridge* was not travelling alone. Several miles behind them the ore carrier *Picket* followed. The two ships kept in constant radio and radar contact.

Freezing ice had now begun to collect on the *Cambridge's* steel body. Havoc was reigning inside the floating vessel. Glasses crashed to the floor, breaking into a million pieces. Books flew from shelves. The crew struggled to stay on foot as the ship bounced from side to side. Chairs scooted across the floors, slamming into the men below.

The captain stood on the bridge watching the ice clumps forming on the window pane. The rain beat on the freighter, hitting the steel sides like bullets. Waves swept over the

Cambridge the instant they hit her broad sides, encasing her in a thick, glossy coating. It was impossible to walk on her decks.

The mighty arms of Lake Superior picked the freighter up like a strong man lifting barbells. Twisting and turning as if to free herself from this death grip, the vessel's steel structure screamed in protest. Peering through the aft windows and looking down the sleek body entombed in ice, the captain wondered how long this lady could endure these mighty blows. No matter how strong and flexible she had been built, there was a limit to her endurance. Never had he seen seas like these! Never so violent had Lake Superior appeared to him!

Word reached him from below. The *Cambridge* was taking on water. Sending a radio signal across the waters, he informed the *Picket* he was having difficulty and to please keep near. The answer came back. They would tag along, keeping communication open.

Once more, the *Cambridge* was lifted high above the water. Again the crew and captain braced themselves, as she slammed back down, waves washing over her. The decisive blow came when she was slapped broadside by an awesome wave, ripping her huge steel frame in two. Then, with one giant swallow, she slipped to the bottom of Lake Superior's belly.

Emily, fingers frozen, her face tingling with the bitter cold, returned to the warmth of her cabin, her task having been completed. She had to hurry if she was going to make it to the Soo in time to see Matthew.

Suddenly the radio blatted out: *"We interrupt this broadcast to bring you this special news bulletin!"* Emily stopped dead in her tracks. *"We have just been informed by the Coast Guard that the 'Harrison P. Cambridge' has sunk off the shores of Lake Superior near Whitefish Point. It is feared all hands are lost. Please stay tuned for further details."* Emily listened as the bulletin was once more repeated.

She ran out of her cabin and raced down to the shore, battling the forceful wind. She gazed into the rain-pelted water but saw nothing. She ran back to her car, jumped in, started the engine, then raced down the drive and down to the point. Leaving the car door open and the motor running, she sprang from the car. Struggling against the tempest, she made her way, half-running, half-walking. The force of the wind knocked her down, causing her to crawl the remaining distance. The sand and snow cut into her exposed skin. The massive waves beating upon the shore sprayed her as she reached the water's edge. Ice began to form in her hair and eyebrows.

Mournfully, the foghorn sounded its signal. How long she stood there, she wasn't aware. Her clothing was soaked to her skin but she felt nothing. Somewhere out in that freezing frenzy was her Matthew. *Dead... dead!* It rang in her ears. Soaked, cold and tired, she made her way back home.

Darkness filled Emily's cabin. The winds shook the house with a moaning sound as if crying in sympathy for her lost loved one. The cold began to creep in as she sat in a chair by the wood stove. The last flames had flickered out. There was no strength or desire in her body to build a new fire. Soaked and in shock, no tears fell from her eyes.

Her heart had been shattered, each sharp piece sending acute pain so severe she could hardly breath. Intensifying anguish fanned throughout her entire body. Even the steady beating of her heart hurt. "Why didn't it stop?" she wondered. "How can it keep beating when it's so broken?"

Could she ever look upon Lake Superior again? How would she be able to bear gazing upon the lake, knowing it was Matthew's final resting place? The thought of him lying in that cold watery grave was more than she could endure. One thought penetrated her mind: *"Escape before daylight!"*

* * * * * * * * *

Emily left her cabin before dawn. Snow was falling and had covered the world in a beautiful white robe. She noticed it not. She'd told no one of her departure. Not even Clem. After packing a few things she had just walked out, locking the door behind her. She couldn't bear to remain there with the knowledge that she'd never see Matthew's ship round the point again. She had no destination, no purpose in life. She only wanted to get as far away from there as she could.

As she drove toward Paradise she thought about how the town would be filled with the news of the *Cambridge* that morning. Emily didn't want to hear it. She didn't want to talk about it or even think about it. The door to her heart was barred and locked forever. She had loved and lost. She had died once again.

CHAPTER TWELVE

BY the time Emily reached Paradise the roads were snow covered and slippery. At this hour Paradise looked like any other sleepy little town in the Upper Peninsula. Everyone was snug and safe in their homes. There was no evidence of the tragic events that had taken place a few hours earlier on Lake Superior.

Emily made one brief stop at the post office, where she slipped two envelopes into the slot of the big blue mail box outside of the building. One was her resignation of her position to study Lake Superior. She couldn't face looking at the lake, let alone study about it. The other was to Clem. It was brief, telling him she was leaving and asking him to look after her home. He knew where the key was to her cabin. She didn't know if or when she would be back. Neither envelope carried a return address. Silently, she slipped out of town.

As the wind picked up snowflakes flew into the headlights of her car, creating a hypnotic effect. Exhaustion was taking over as her body tensed from the storm raging outside as well as inside her heart. As she crossed the bridge over the mouth of the Tahquamenon River she was thankful it was dark so she couldn't see Lake Superior on her left. Highway 123 stretched out before her. The only sound Emily heard was the windshield wipers beating out a steady rhythm.

Mile after mile she drove, through the town of Trout Lake and onto south Highway I-75. Approaching the Mackinaw Bridge, she pulled up to the toll booth to pay her fare. Until now she had always thrilled to cross the five-mile expanse of bridge over the Straits of Mackinaw. Today it held no meaning for her, except to get as far away from the Upper Peninsula as she could. To stay above the bridge would only bring a daily reminder of the sinking of the *Cambridge*. It would be talked about no matter where in the U.P. she would go. If she could find a small town in lower Michigan, maybe the sinking of a freighter wouldn't be discussed.

Mackinaw City was just waking up as she reached the end of the bridge and pulled onto Nicolet Street. Her gas gauge registered near empty. Pulling into the closest gas station she prayed the attendant wouldn't mention the news she dreaded hearing. As she waited for him to pump the gas she debated in her mind the route she would take — highway or back roads? The lad returned with her change and bid her a good day.

Emily left the gas station, turned right and drove down the Mackinaw Highway, and then onto U.S. 31. The snow covered road was slippery as she drove through the little town of Carp Lake. Her mind was a million miles away as she continued aimlessly through Levering, Pellston, Alanson and then Bay View, lined with its grand old summer homes. Finally she reached Petoskey. Her car seemed to be driving itself as she continued south onto U.S. 131.

As mile after mile went by, the pain in her heart became more raw and needed to be released! Cries of despair would escape her lips and her fist would hit the steering wheel. "Why, God, Why!" She cried out loud as tears flowed from her eyes, almost blinding her. Oh, how she longed to feel Matthew's hand in hers, his arms around her, their cheeks snuggled next to each other, his soft breath fanning her face. She had always wanted to bury her fingers in his hair and tell him how much she loved him! This piercing pain that filled her body and heart made her realize just how deeply she had loved him. These feelings for Matthew were entirely different than the feelings she had thought she'd had for Paul. This sweet awakening in her heart had been true love — an unspoken love. The fact that she would never have any of those feelings, those tender touches or those spoken words, was too much for her fragile frame of mind.

Emily pulled over to the side of the road, laid her head on the steering wheel, and wailed in deep anguished sobs. Totally drained both physically and mentally, she fell asleep.

CHAPTER THIRTEEN

A SHARP RAP on the window startled Emily out of her sleep. Seeing a police officer standing beside her car, she rolled the window down.

"Are you ok, lady?" he questioned.

"Yes, officer, I'm sorry. I pulled off to... to...", she stammered, " ... to rest."

After looking at her license, he bid her a safe trip.

She glanced at her watch and realized she had been traveling for six or seven hours. The snow had stopped falling and there wasn't as much on the ground as when she'd left home. According to her car thermometer it was thirty-nine degrees outside.

Emily sought out the back roads, driving slower, looking

for a small town to stop in. Empty fields ran along each side of the road. Cattle lingered in the mucky dirt. Bales of hay were stacked neatly alongside the barns, and farm houses dotted the landscape.

She approached the tiny village of Dorr, Michigan. The little town had few buildings. One gas station stood on the corner. A barber shop and a post office stood on one side of Main Street. She glanced across the roadway. A bank, hardware store, bar, two small grocery stores, and a restaurant with a sign that read MABEL'S HOME COOKING stood side by side. A grain elevator was grinding corn down the street. A horse hitched in front of the hardware store was waiting patiently for its owner to return.

Emily drove into the gas station to fill up her car. The attendant was a young, smiling man with a home town charm.

"Fill 'er up, Miss?" he asked.

"Yes, please, and could you tell me where I could find a place to stay tonight?"

"Well now, we don't have too many places like that here," he stated. "But if you go over to Mabel's she might be able to help you out for a night or two," he grinned.

Emily paid for the gas, thanked the young man, parked her car along the side of the road and walked across the street to Mabel's. It was an old-fashioned restaurant, dark inside, with well-worn tables and chairs. Scuff marks covered the dark wooden floor. Red and white checked table cloths brought a little brightness to the place.

A few men sat at a round table in the corner. Emily didn't pay much attention to them; her thoughts were still far away. She picked a table on the other side of the room and sat down. She was too tired to care about anything or anyone else. An elderly lady carrying a large bowl of steaming hot vegetable soup approached her. It surprised Emily, for she hadn't ordered anything, let alone talked to anyone.

The woman spoke. "I think you need this, dear, you look exhausted."

Her voice was soft and soothing to Emily's ears. Looking up, she gazed into one of the kindest faces she had seen in a long time. Deep wrinkles covered the woman's entire face. Wisps of gray hair framed her features. Blue eyes behind glasses sparkled as she smiled down on Emily. Emily wanted to cry, but quickly lowered her eyes.

"Thank you," was all she could manage.

"I'm Mable Smith, and you are?" she asked with kindness.

Emily hesitated to reveal her name, but decided no one would know her.

"Emily Kincaid." Her tone was tired, but polite.

"Do you need a place to stay tonight?" she inquired.

Emily had a feeling Mabel already knew the answer to that question.

"Yes, I could use one, I've traveled all day and I'm very tired." Her voice was flat.

"Eat your soup, honey. It'll put strength back in you. I have a place you can stay tonight." And with those words Mabel walked back into the kitchen.

Unbeknownst to Emily, Mabel had been watching her at the gas station when she pulled into town. Mabel was a pretty good judge of character. As soon as she'd laid eyes on Emily, she'd detected something was heavy on this young girl's heart. Mabel had noticed how spent the young girl appeared—how her shoulders stooped, and her feet dragged. It was verified when Emily walked into the restaurant and Mabel looked into those eyes that were red from crying. She wouldn't pry as to the trouble Emily was in. Mabel had a reputation for taking in strangers and feeding and caring for them. Maybe in time the girl would share her story.

* * * * * *

When Emily woke up the next morning she wondered where she was. She sat up to get her bearings. Slowly it came to her. Mabel had taken Emily to her home, showed her to a room and run a hot bath for her. The room was very old-fashioned, but comfortable. Faded wallpaper, splashed with big pink roses, covered the walls. Well-worn green carpet lay on the floor. Old lace curtains covered the two windows and were pulled back, letting in sunlight. A candy-striped pink and white canopy covered her big four-poster bed. The scent of lavender filled the room. Emily lay back down and gazed across the room to the large old dresser and mirror. At that moment the events of the past flooded her mind. A feeling of extreme dread descended upon her, a weight so heavy it threatened to suffocate her.

A soft knock sounded on the door. She looked toward it and softly called, "Come in."

Mabel entered carrying a small tray with toast and tea on it. "Good morning, Emily, did you sleep well?" Mabel asked.

Emily sat up in bed. "Yes, how long did I sleep?" she

asked.

"Oh about twelve hours. You were really tuckered out."

"Thank you for taking me in," Emily said with a catch in her voice. "It was kind of you to do so, and very kind to bring me breakfast."

"Oh, think nothing of it. I love having young people around." She smiled.

"I will be leaving this afternoon," Emily stated.

Looking Emily in the eye, Mable said, "I could use some help in the restaurant and you're welcome to stay here with me." Panic gripped Emily's heart. If she stayed would this woman pry into her past?

Mabel saw the fear in Emily's face. "This girl is afraid of something," she pondered to herself. Quickly, Mabel added, "You are free to leave anytime you want to, honey, but it would be a joy to have you around, and I sure could use the help. When you're finished with breakfast, come over to the restaurant." And she left Emily alone.

It was mid-afternoon when Emily entered the restaurant. Mabel was in the kitchen, and when she saw Emily she motioned for her to come behind the counter and join her. Mabel was stirring a large pot of homemade beef stew. With a little fear and trembling, Emily spoke. "I would like to stay for a while, Ma'am. I'm not sure how long, and I prefer not to work out in front, if that's okay with you."

"That will be fine," she smiled. "But please call me Mabel, otherwise I won't know who you're talking to."

A pattern began to develop for Emily as the days turned into weeks and the weeks into months. She kept to herself except to spend some evenings with Mabel in her cozy home around a comfortable fire in the stone fireplace. Emily had discovered a little park, just down the road from where she stayed. A narrow little stream of water called Rabbit River cut through the park. It bubbled and danced, making a soft soothing sound. A small wooden bridge allowed crossing from the park to a farmer's field. Each morning Emily would walk there, stand on the wooden structure with her arms leaning on the railing, and listen to the flow of the small stream. Snow flakes would gently fall upon her covered head. Crisp, cold morning air turned her cheeks a cherry red. Here she would pour her broken heart out to God, for there she found the strength to enter the day and live through the memories that were always present in her heart and mind.

Emily had always been a person who loved to walk, rain or shine. On the days the restaurant was closed, she would bundle up in her boots, scarf, hat and gloves and venture out into the cold winter weather. She craved solitude, walking for miles along the lonely country roads, feeling the cold bite into her face as the snowflakes covered her head and shoulders. She would be gone for hours, until she could walk no more. Upon her return Mabel had a chair for her by the fireplace and a hot meal waiting.

Thanksgiving and Christmas came and went. Emily had no desire to celebrate either of them. Having no family of her own, Mabel was content to spend both days quietly dozing in her chair.

As spring approached robins returned, heralding their arrival with soft trilling songs. Splashes of yellow daffodils, red tulips and purple hyacinths began to bloom outside the door. The morning air was filled with the sweet scent of rain gently falling to earth. The sight and sound cut deep into Emily's heart. It seemed like so long ago when she thrilled to these early signs of spring. Would she, could she, ever find pleasure in them again?

After awakening one morning with a start, Emily realized she'd had a vivid dream of Matthew! Laying still for fear she would lose the vision, her mind retraced every detail of it. Realizing it was only a dream caused her much pain. But something stirred inside her breast. A strong desire engulfed her. She wanted to be near Matthew. She needed to be near him!

When she entered Mabel's kitchen, the dear lady had her back to Emily. Before Emily could say anything, Mabel spoke. "So, you'll be leaving today?" she asked.

Emily stood there silent. *"How did she know?"* she wondered, and she voiced the question to Mabel.

"Oh, you've been more restless lately, Emily, and I knew the day was soon at hand."

It touched Emily's heart that this lady who had become so dear to her in the past few months could read her so. Mabel turned around and saw the tears in Emily's eyes. She crossed the room, took Emily in her arms, and spoke soothing words to her. "My dear, don't cry. I've enjoyed having you here, and it's helped an old lady get through another winter. I have the restaurant and that does help, but you've just been so special to have around." She quickly turned around and wiped her tears on her apron.

"You've been so good to me," Emily hesitated, fighting back her tears. "I knew my leaving would be hard on you... and me," she said, "but I need to go back home. There's something I need to do. I haven't been able to talk about the deep hurt I've been feeling from something that happened before I arrived here. Someone..." she found the words stuck in her throat, as the pain in her heart increased. "Someone," she continued, "very dear to me... died, and..." It was the first time she had audibly spoken those words to another person. Before she could finish, Mabel turned around and gathered Emily in her frail arms. They clung to each other for a brief moment, said their goodbyes, then Emily left as the rain continued to fall.

CHAPTER FOURTEEN

WHEN EMILY arrived at Whitefish Point and pulled into her driveway she found her cabin was just as she had left it. Emily stepped from her car and breathed deeply of the warm fresh air. She entered the cabin and then stopped and gazed around the room. Warmth filled her heart at the sight of neatly stacked mail on her table. The electricity was still on and there was no evidence of winter damage anywhere. She stood in the middle of the room and spoke out loud. "Dear, sweet, Clem, you did a good job!" It was as if he had sensed her homecoming and had everything in readiness.

Emily went in search of the hammer and crowbar that would release the boards from her windows. As she stepped outside she noticed black heavy clouds moving in. A storm was approaching. With eager fingers she pried the boards loose and stood them against the cabin. Just as she was finishing, large drops of rain began to fall and the rumbling of thunder was advancing upon her.

Light now flooded the cabin as she once more entered. Her eyes rested upon the picture of the clipper ship and the phantom sea captain. For a brief moment her heart stopped beating. Turning from its view, she sat down at the oak table. As she sorted through the stacks of mail, Emily's fingers came to rest on an envelope with familiar writing. It was Matthew's! Could she open it? Slowly, with caution, so as not to tear the paper inside, she opened it. She held the letter in her hand as if it was something sacred. Slowly, she began to read:

Dear Emily,

I am writing this letter to you in the quiet of my cabin. I cannot hold what is in my heart any longer. I must speak of my feelings to you. I love you, Emily, and have for some time now. I would be honored if you would be my wife. I have not had the courage to speak to you of this before. I wanted to the day we spent at the park, but time wouldn't allow it. I was secretly glad I couldn't speak to you then, for fear of your answer. If your answer is no, then I will steel myself to accept it, and will learn to fight these feelings I have for you. I must know now, Emily, for I can't go on this way any longer. If the answer is no, I will leave you be and will put my entire life into my work as I have done in the past. But if you should say yes, Emily, you will make me a very happy man. Please answer soon!

Faithfully yours,
Matthew C.

Emily sat staring at the letter, then looked at the date it was mailed. It was postmarked one day before he had sailed on his fateful journey. If only the letter had come sooner. She would have been comforted with the knowledge that she had answered him back; that indeed she had loved him, and it would be her honor to be his wife. The letter had come too late.

The approaching storm had stopped right over Emily's cabin. Resounding claps of thunder shook the windows, doors and furnishings of her tiny abode. Blinding flashes of lightning filled the room as torrents of rain fell upon the cabin roof. It was as if nature herself was sympathizing with her, for at that moment a loud cry of anguish escaped her lips, and the flood waters broke forth from the locked doors of her heart, as well as the sky. The silent grief she bore for Matthew's death could not be confined any longer. Sprawling across the table, arms stretched out before her, she clung to it as if it would give her comfort, while water flowed from her eyes, nose and mouth. Envelopes scattered to the floor, falling soundlessly. Great sobs came from the depths of her spirit as Emily's soul was wrung from her with each peal of thunder overhead.

"Matthew, Matthew, M A T T H E W!"

The storm slacked and moved on. The remaining sound of falling rain filled the tomb-like cabin. Emily opened her eyes and focused on a small box wrapped in brown paper and tied with string. It was resting near her hand. She lifted her head and stared at it. After wiping her face with a tissue, she gingerly picked up the package and studied it. The handwriting was unfamiliar. She ripped off the paper, opened the box and dumped the contents on the table. A letter fell out, along with a gold ring on a gold chain. Emily recoiled from the object! It was Matthew's ring! Frantically, she searched the paper for a postmark! It was dated one week after the *Cambridge* went down. With trembling fingers she unfolded the letter and read:

Dear Miss Kincaid,

I am writing to you regarding a Captain Matthew Christian who is a patient in our hospital. He is a very sick man with a fever of 105 degrees. He has called your name several times in his delirium. We didn't know where to contact next of kin, but found your name and address in his belongings. We thought this ring might have some significance to you, and we are sending it in hopes you will contact us. If you would, please contact our hospital. Our address and phone number are below. Please call as soon as you receive this letter, for the captain is gravely ill.

Sincerely,

Cynthia Ryan R.N.

"What have I done? Oh... what have I done?" Emily moaned out loud. If she had stayed would she have seen him again? Now he could be dead. This letter was written months ago, after his freighter went down.

Emily rushed to the phone and picked up the receiver, preparing to dial the number. Her phone was dead! Her head began to move from side to side. "Matthew, oh Matthew. Did you survive the shipwreck, and I didn't know it?" she cried out loud. She had to get out of this cabin. The atmosphere was suffocating her. Heedless of the rain still falling, she rushed outside. Her dry clothes soaked up the water like a thirsty sponge, causing them to cling to her body as she made her way toward the shore. Just coming up over the incline from the beach was a man in a yellow slicker, his captain's cap pulled down over his eyes. He had a walking stick in his hand and was bent into the rain. Emily stopped as the figure approached. As he lifted his head she recognized Clem. Dashing toward him, she flung herself into his arms. His soaked beard was soggy against her cheek. His frail, thin arms encircled her.

"Girlie, Girlie, we thought you be dead. Why didn't you tell me where you were going?"

"Oh, Clem, I'm sorry, but I wasn't thinking clearly. Clem, what has happened to Matthew? Do you know?" She wailed.

Gently releasing his hold on her, he stepped aside. Looking past Clem, Emily saw another man standing just a few feet from them. His wavy dark hair, flecked with silver, glistened with droplets as water trickled down his noble nose and onto his chin. Unlike Clem, he wore no yellow slicker, but had chosen to let the rain soak into his love-starved body. He stood with his hands beside him, his eyes locked into Emily's!

A cry escaped her lips, "Matthew!"

He opened his arms toward her and she flew into them. His arms crushed her to him as their bodies clung to each other. Showering her face, eyes, and finally her lips with wet kisses, he devoured her.

Big tears cascaded down Clem's cheeks and nestled into his beard as he turned from them and slowly made his way to Emily's cabin. He would put a pot of coffee on and wait until this glad reunion was over.

"Matthew," she breathed into his wet neck, "What happened? Didn't your ship go down?"

"I have so much to tell you, Emily. Yes, the *Cambridge* went down with all hands on board. But I wasn't on that ship. The day I called you to let you know we were about to set sail I became violently ill, collapsed on board, and had to be taken off the boat on a stretcher. My company wanted to get that shipment through so they hired a temporary captain until I could get better. I wasn't aware the *Cambridge* had sunk until several weeks later. When I recovered I tried to get in touch with you but I couldn't find you. I came to Clem, and he didn't know your whereabouts either. He has been very kind to me, Emily. He took me in for the winter. I had no heart to go back to sailing until I knew what had happened to you. I tried to find you but you did a good job of hiding yourself." He smiled.

"Oh Matthew," Emily answered, "when I heard that you were dead, or thought you were dead, I couldn't stay here another day. I couldn't stand the thought of seeing another freighter pass this point, knowing you weren't on it. So I left."

"Emily, I wrote to you... asking you a question."

"I know," she answered him before he could go on. "I just read it this morning. My answer is yes, Matthew! I love you and I want to be your wife."

Looking deep into her eyes, he voiced the question on his mind. "Emily, will it bother you that I am older than you?"

"Does it bother you," she quizzed back, "that I'm younger than you?"

A chuckle broke forth from his lips. "No, darling, it doesn't bother me. We have sailed some rough seas. I think we can handle any other storms that may come our way."

Putting her hands into his thick dark hair, for she had always wanted to feel it, she pulled his face down to hers and their lips met.

The storm clouds parted and rays of sunshine broke through, descending to the water. A rainbow arched the sky. The huge form of a thousand-foot freighter poked its nose from behind the trees as it rounded the point.

Clem peered out of the window and wiped a tear from his eye. Scratching his beard, he watched Matthew and Emily, lost in each other's love.

"By gum... I think the captain has found his safe harbor!"

About the author...

MELODY BERG is a native of Michigan. Having been born and raised in Grand Rapids, she now resides at Whitefish Point where her time is divided between work, writing and her garden. A wife and mother of two, her love of literature and poetry developed during childhood, thanks to the encouragement and influence of her mother. Melody's life-long goal of publishing a novel resulted first in this book and later in a second volume, ROUND BY THE POINT. In addition, she is the author of numerous short stories. Summer vacations and the ultimate building of a house at Whitefish Point have fed her love of the water, and especially of Lake Superior. Following the death of her husband, she and her dog relocated to Whitefish Point where, in addition to writing, she works as a docent at The Great Lakes Shipwreck Museum.

Made in the USA
Lexington, KY
17 September 2017